The Secret Obituary Writer

The Secret
Obituary Writer

Amy Martinsen

Cover design by Tracy Anderson (TracyAndersonPhoto.com)

ISBN-13: 978-1-73431-483-0

First published by Walnut Springs Press (ISBN-13: 978-1-59992-962-0) in 2016.

Obituary [noun]: an announcement that someone has died, published in a newspaper in the form of a brief biography.
Oxford English Dictionary

Acknowledgments

My deepest gratitude to Molly, for doing our family history and finding me all these great names. To Allison, for helping me see myself as a writer. To Mrs. Waters, for being such a wonderful high school English teacher and dear friend. To Linda, for giving me a chance. And to Gordy, for the miracle of finding this manuscript on the side of the road and bringing every page of it back to me.

One

Obituaries should tell the truth, or at least reveal the cause of death. That way we don't imagine all kinds of awful scenarios. The truth is less frightening—or at least I used to think so.

At a time when the newspaper delivery business was taking its last breath, the *Cutlip Currier* chugged along as steadily as the eighty-five-year-old heart of Zumba instructor Gladys Ziggler. I didn't really know Gladys yet, but the fact that she was so fit at her age made me hope I would have the chance to write her obituary and find out more about her.

My printer spit out the latest obit. It was straightforward, filled with abandoned dreams and unaccomplished goals that until now had been known only to the deceased. Of course, readers would learn just how the man perished. That was intriguing in and of itself, but it was dead people's hidden obsessions and secret lives that provided me with job security. Yet even Mayor Poindexter's shocking revelation about his secret life as a romance novelist was nothing compared to what was waiting for me in my email inbox. I just didn't know it yet.

After removing the stack of papers from the printer, I added them to the others, making a hefty pile. I pulled a black garbage bag around the pile, grabbed my car keys, and headed for the door. It was nearly 3:00 AM. A full moon lit the night sky. May had been surprisingly warm for Cutlip, with balmy air that reminded me of July. I climbed into my car to drive the three blocks to the latest drop-off spot. We regularly changed the place, just to be safe.

All the houses along the road were dark. Tree branches rustled in the breeze, creating macabre shadows that might have seemed scary if I hadn't lived in Cutlip for all of my twenty years. The town is about forty-five minutes east of Missoula, where I attend the University of Montana. I'd planned to move closer to campus, but my parents needed someone to housesit. They went to Toronto, Canada, for my dad's year-long medical sabbatical. Since my two older brothers are married and live out of state, I was the obvious choice. Not only didn't I mind, but it was great to have a free place to live while attending college, holding down a part-time job as a high school math tutor, and, of course, writing secret (READ: special) obituaries.

As I approached the third block, I turned off my car's headlights. Seconds later I pulled onto the shoulder of the road and rolled down the window. Mr. Jonas stood waiting exactly where his email had indicated—between the tree and the dumpster by the vacant house east of the grocery store. Mr. Jonas, a widower for many years, had no children and was now married to his newspaper business.

I'd tried forever to get him to some of the church socials or single mingles, but to no avail. He had once been an active member of the Cutlip Community Church—the church attended by most of the town's residents, including my family—but when his wife died, he quit attending. Bringing him back to the fold had been the focus of more youth-group service projects than I could count. He obviously loved the constant flow of treats, but he had yet to darken the doorway of the church building. He and I finally came to an understanding: I quit trying to find him a fine Christian woman, and he quit trying to set me up with his nephew Leonard, the one with the lazy eye.

Mr. Jonas shifted his weight from one foot to the other, his tall, thin frame casting a long shadow in the moonlight. I glanced at the time on my car's dashboard. *Uh-oh, it's 3:02!* He always got nervous when I was late. He reached the passenger-side door before I could turn off the engine.

"Mornin', Lizzy Girl. How'd it go this time?" Mr. Jonas had called me Lizzy Girl for as long as I can remember. My name is Elizabeth Ann Langston, but almost everyone knows me as Lizzy.

"Nothing too exciting in this one, but it's still good. Got an email at home that's lookin' pretty weird."

Mr. Jonas leaned his gray head into the window. "I like the sound of that. Let me know when it's ready." He opened the car door, tossed a wad of cash onto the seat, and wrestled the huge bag of obituaries into his arms. "Thanks, Lizzy. Drive home safe and get some rest."

"See you later," I said, then started the motor. Once I'd turned the car around, I glanced back and saw my boss disappear around the side of the dumpster. Drop-off meetings were always brief. We didn't want to be seen, of course, but even more importantly, Mr. Jonas had to rush to get the obituaries to the newspaper carriers, who would fold them and insert one in each copy of today's *Cutlip Currier,* between sections A and B. That's right next to the regular obituaries—the ones that make every dead person sound wonderful and perfect.

I knew the obituary-stuffing procedure by heart. I should—I'm the one who started it.

Eli Poindexter
1943–2013

Mayor Eli Poindexter, beloved civic leader of Cutlip, died of colon cancer at the age of seventy. Mayor Poindexter was president of the Chamber of Commerce for a decade before being elected mayor and serving for three consecutive terms. A popular speaker at Toastmaster breakfasts, he was awarded the Golden Gavel Award an unprecedented three times. He was also the favored recipient of Sophronia Cutlip's famed holiday fruit cake every Christmas, a clear sign of his distinguished position in the community.

While these offices and awards were important to Mr. Poindexter, something else made him equally proud—something that for obvious reasons had to remain a secret until now. Eli Poindexter is none other than the acclaimed and prolific romance novelist Tillman Bobo. Mr. Poindexter has published eighty-eight romance novels under this nom de plume. Knowing his time was short, the mayor wrote to me, requesting a post-mortem reveal of his hidden talent.

And talented he was. He was awarded the Romantic Novel of the Year (aka RoNA) Award for his wildly popular novel A Rogue for All Seasons. *He also received a RITA Golden Heart Winner for the same book.* The Love Interest of Wolf Mane Lane *earned him the Romantic Novelists' Association (aka RNA's) prestigious Rona Rose Award. But dearest to Eli's/Tillman's heart was the RoNA Love Story of the Year Award garnered by his romantic tale* The Ne'er-Do-Well of Nehawka. *Last but certainly not least, the covers of several Tillman Bobo novels were graced with a photograph of Fabio, an honor of which only a select number of romance writers can boast.*

Mayor Poindexter loved the town of Cutlip. Therefore, as Tillman Bobo, he established the Fabio-Bobo Scholarship Fund to be awarded to an up-and-coming romance novelist. The scholarship will be awarded each year to the winner of the Fabio-Bobo Writing Contest, the committee for which will be headed by Alice Clonts, the town librarian. Mayor Poindexter also donated a copy of all eighty-eight Tillman Bobo novels to the library. I was instructed to send a notification regarding this donation to Ms. Clonts, who seemed both shocked and delighted in her response. She wrote, "Although I haven't finished unboxing the books, I did take a peek at A Cad Walks at Midnight. *The people of Cutlip are in for a real treat!"*

Two

When I was twelve, I wanted an iPod so bad my teeth ached. Dad was one of the few family doctors in Cutlip, so we didn't live in poverty or anything close to it, but my parents would never give me something as expensive as an iPod. I would need to earn the money for it. The old standby of babysitting was extremely competitive in our community, with thirteen girls my age. So it came down to who had produced the most elaborate babysitting kit in Girl Scouts. The babysitting kit, a box containing crafts and toys that would hopefully entertain even the most difficult of children, was the brain child of the Corban triplets—Riley, Mackenzie, and Brianna. They belonged to a nice Mormon family, whose mom not only owned a beauty supply store, but also ran a successful scrapbooking business out of her home. Their dad managed a Dollar Tree. Anyway, of course the Corbans had the best babysitting kits and therefore got all the easy, high-paying jobs. That left the low-paying, undesirable ones for the rest of us girls to fight over.

After several disgusting attempts at house cleaning and lawn mowing, I landed at the office of Mr. Abraham Jonas. He owned and ran the *Cutlip Currier* and had posted a help-wanted ad for carriers. As the coach of my T-ball team, Mr. Jonas knew about my strong overhand throw. Plus, I had a reliable Cruiser bike with a basket. Delivering papers couldn't be any harder than cleaning toilets or enduring the effects of mowing over dried dog poop. I applied to be a newspaper carrier and was hired on the spot. Mr. Jonas seemed intrigued that a girl would aspire to what at the time was considered a boy's job, at least in our community. Neither of us knew I would someday save his business.

As I was learning the ropes of newspaper delivery, the Cutlip Community Church's woman's group asked my mom to look in on Loretta Campbell. After all, everyone had to take their turn. Loretta must have been born old and grumpy—we couldn't imagine her any other way. I often went with my mom to visit the lady, and each time we left her house felt like being released from prison. I actually think my mom took me for protection.

We always tried to cheer up Loretta, but nothing seemed to make it through her fortress of negativity . . . until that one pivotal moment. The church had solicited volunteers to bring dinner to Loretta, and on my mom's scheduled day she was running behind, so the task fell to me. The elderly woman always expected dinner by 5:00 and would leave the front door unlocked.

I'll never forget the feeling of walking into her home alone, armed with nothing but a tuna noodle casserole adorned with crushed potato chips. Loretta glared at me from her perch on the sofa as I walked through her living room into the kitchen. After placing the casserole on a hot pad, I squared my shoulders and marched back to the living room to "sit and have a visit," as my mother had firmly instructed. I sat opposite Loretta, crossed my legs, and folded my arms—I had my own fortress thing going on.

Her gaze took all this in and then softened a bit. "How was your day at school, Lizzy?" she asked, actually smiling.

It was the first time I'd seen her produce anything close to a smile, not to mention the first time she'd ever spoken to me. I didn't think she even knew my name.

"Fine," I answered, feeling I was walking into a trap.

"Tell me about your teachers."

"Uh, well, my homeroom teacher is Mr. Figley. He color-coordinates his shirts with the days of the week. Monday is always blue, Tuesday is red, Wednesday is purple, Thursday is green, and Friday is gray." I knew I was rambling, but nervousness kept me going. "He wears the same pair of pants all week. The whole class knows because we track the chalk marks on his rear end. He looks a little creepy because he has pasty-white skin but a ton of black arm hair. He lives with his mother and her poodle, Love Muffin. Oh, and we're pretty sure Mr. Figley eats raw onions for breakfast every day."

When Loretta Campbell laughed out loud at my comments, her face was transformed. She appeared younger, her eyes brighter. She asked me more questions, about school, then about my friends and my paper route, and I answered her in my blunt, twelve-year-old way. By the way, my mom was working with me on that whole "blunt" thing, trying to help me become what she referred to as "sweetly subtle."

Over the next few months, Loretta and I became friends. She told me about her life growing up during the Great Depression, how little her family had but how happy they were until her dad was killed in a mining accident. Things were never happy after that, Loretta confided. Later, she fell in love with a guy named John. He asked her to marry him, but she kept putting him off. Then he went to war and got killed. She told me that her misery and orneriness were brought on by her regrets about John.

On my early-morning paper route, I would sometimes attach a funny note to Loretta's newspaper. If I had time, I would stop by on my way home from school to see if she liked the note. One afternoon I'd already planned to stop by, but an urgent feeling made me want to run all the way to her house. And I did.

Loretta always kept the back door unlocked during the day, so I hurried into the house and made my way to the front room. I found her lying on the floor, looking gray. Her eyes were glassy, but they focused when she saw me. She reached out her hand. I took it and knelt beside her.

"Are you okay, Loretta? Did you fall? Did you have a spell? Can I help you up? I should call my mom, or 9-1-1," I said in one breath. She pulled my hand to her chest.

"Lizzy, listen to me." Her voice sounded breathy as she struggled to inhale. "I'm not who people think I am. They don't know me like you do." She stopped and tried to swallow.

"I should go get someone!" I was afraid to be there with her, but more afraid to leave her.

"No, Lizzy, please listen to me," she insisted, gripping my hand harder. "Write an obituary about me. They'll do the regular one, but I want you to write what I've told you and put it in the papers on your route." She stopped and closed her eyes. For a moment I thought she had died, but her warm hand still held mine.

"I was afraid to marry John, afraid to commit," Miss Campbell continued. "I missed so much. I never had a family, never had love." Her voice was weakening so I leaned closer. "Lizzy, regrets make you grumpy. Let them go. Don't be afraid."

Her hand went limp and her chest stilled. I had never seen anyone die before and had imagined all kinds of horrible things, but this wasn't horrible at all. A peaceful, light feeling settled around me. I had heard people at church talk about experiences like this, but I had never understood until I knelt next to Miss Campbell and held her hand as she crossed over into the Great Beyond.

That evening, after all the commotion was over and I had assured my parents for the tenth time that I was okay, I wrote the obituary:

Miss Loretta Campbell was not who you think she was. She could be cheerful and smile and laugh, though not many people had the privilege of seeing this side of her. She was a happy little girl until her father died. As a young woman, Miss Campbell fell in love with a man named John, but she was too afraid of commitment to marry him. When he went to war and got killed, she realized her mistake and felt she had lost her one chance for happiness.

She acted grumpy and ornery because she realized she had allowed fear to rule her life. She lived with regrets she couldn't let go of. Miss Campbell wanted everyone to understand this about her.

I had sixty-five people on my route, so I printed out sixty-five obituaries and snuck them into the next day's delivery. Although I did it anonymously, I knew I might be found out, but at least I had honored Loretta's last wish.

Over the next few weeks I watched and listened, picking up comments that broke through the polite surface of adult whispers. "Who knew?" "Who was John?" "What horrible things to live through!" I felt happy and important for helping change how people remembered Loretta.

I never dreamed anyone else would want the same thing done for them. When Mr. Jonas showed up at my front door one evening, I just knew I'd been found out. Now I would lose my job. *Kiss your iPod goodbye,* I grumbled silently.

He asked to speak with my parents and me together. I very nearly threw up. After the four of us sat down, Mr. Jonas said he thought I was the one who had written and inserted Loretta Campbell's "special" obituary into the paper. Over the last few weeks, he had received several requests for this same type of obituary, and he couldn't ignore the business opportunity. Right then and there, in front of my mom and dad, he offered me a job as a secret obituary writer. I almost fell over with relief.

As my parents sat there with their jaws on the floor, I accepted the position. We decided Mr. Jonas would screen the requests. I would write and print the obituaries, then secretly give them back to him. He would make copies available to the carriers of the *Cutlip Currier.* Whether or not they inserted them into the papers was their choice. This arrangement allowed for a small bit of protection. If someone got upset, Mr. Jonas could claim he didn't put the obituary in the paper. Equally important was my complete anonymity. But nobody complained, and when I turned eighteen, we set up a public email account, 2BUnderstood@ hotmail.com, in honor of Miss Campbell, where anyone could request my services.

Sometimes requests came from people who knew they were dying and wanted to get more personal than would be appropriate or allowed in a traditional obituary. Family members, especially the caregivers of the ill or deceased, would often email information to me. I knew most of the people I wrote about and they knew me, but they didn't realize I was the secret obituary writer. That was exactly the way Mr. Jonas and I wanted it.

Three

Over the years there were a few failed attempts to discover my identity, but most Cutlip residents accepted my anonymity. What once was a thin line of protection had turned into a novelty. The common thread of the feedback about the secret obituaries? The people of Cutlip did *not* want this messed with. They wanted the "special" obituaries—the more the merrier. When we received complaints, they usually came from people *not* receiving my obituaries. Since it was solely up to the carriers to insert the folded obituaries into the newspaper, these complaints were given with a sense of desperation and shame because they revealed a poor relationship between recipient and carrier. And no *Cutlip Currier* subscriber wanted that.

Most people don't even know their newspaper carriers, so those who delivered the *Cutlip Currier* definitely had it good. In other communities, a customer might find a Christmas card inserted in his or her copy of the newspaper during the holiday season, but the signed name would soon be forgotten. And since more and more people chose to receive their news in digital format, carriers were becoming a thing of the past. But not in Cutlip.

Just about every community supports and brags about their high school sports teams, bands, and track teams. Cutlip did too, of course, but members of those groups couldn't match the elite status of our newspaper carriers. As the popularity of the obituaries grew and subscribers understood it was the carriers who made sure the obits got delivered, the carriers practically became celebrities overnight. Instead of the annual Christmas tip for their carriers, many newspaper subscribers now gave monthly bonuses in the form of gift cards for Dairy Queen and 7-Eleven. Dilly Bars and Slurpees flowed freely.

It became a competition among subscribers to see who could have the happiest and therefore the most loyal carrier. Gift cards for convenience stores and fast-food restaurants escalated to free passes to laser-tag venues and water parks. Random gifts, new bike seats and baskets, and faster, better tires—to make for a speedier delivery— were delivered to the carriers' homes. I had an iPod in no time flat and enjoyed riding around listening to tunes while sipping a Slurpee and snacking on Flamin' Hot Cheetos.

When a carrier quit, usually to go away to college, it was like a feeding frenzy to fill the position. Mr. Jonas never had to advertise for carriers. The position's availability was known well in advance, and all my boss had to do was consult his long waiting list of applicants. Some kids waited years to be carriers. Some positions were passed down from one sibling to the other. It was a huge competition to see if an applicant could get bumped up on the list. Mr. Jonas dragged the hiring process out as long as he could, enjoying the bribes and gifts.

I quit delivering newspapers after a few years, mainly to keep my obituary writing anonymous. A classmate, Bruce Owens, filled my spot when I recommended him to Mr. Jonas. Out of gratitude, Bruce gave me his dessert at school lunch every day for two months.

These happy memories played through my mind as I sat in front of my computer to check my obituary email. I had slept for a few hours after the 3:00 AM drop-off, but still fought to stay awake during Advanced Calculus. On the way home from the university, I stopped to get an extra-large Diet Pepsi.

There was still just one unread message in my inbox, from Betty Whipple. The subject line read "Oliver Moore's death." I clicked on the message and read:

> *Ollie didn't die falling off his tractor. I know you are anonymous and safe—please don't say anything. Even though no laws were broken, at least that I know of, I needed to tell someone. The guilt is giving me indigestion.*

Intriguing! Mr. Moore's passing had occurred a few months previously. The quiet, elderly widower had lost his wife Nedra to breast cancer about a decade before. Their children, all married, lived out of state. I crossed paths with Oliver a few times at church and was impressed with his starched shirts and shined shoes. He was a handsome man, a veteran who still carried himself with the squared shoulders and sure gait of a soldier. He lived on the outskirts of town and still farmed a few acres. Someone found Oliver lying dead next to his tractor, apparently having suffered a heart attack while driving the vehicle. At least that was the information in the newspaper article honoring deceased veterans. Mr. Jonas, himself a Vietnam vet, had come up with the idea for the tribute, but one of the reporters had researched and written it.

Neither Mr. Moore nor his family had requested a secret obituary, so this was the first information I had received. Betty Whipple, a widow in her sixties, was an active member of the Red Hat Society, an organization for older women that encouraged flamboyant dress and other behavior not typical of older widows. One look at Mr. Moore and you wouldn't guess he and Mrs. Whipple would be friends, but what did I know.

In the past I had received explanations about how someone died, but never before had someone contradicted the cause of death. My first instinct was to go to the police, but if no law had been broken, I wasn't going to risk giving up my anonymity for what was possibly a secret romance that could be, at the very least, a surprise to Mr. Moore's family. I decided to wait and see if Mrs. Whipple's guilt-induced indigestion forced her to contact me again.

Four

The sound of a door closing downstairs broke through my sleep. *Just Hannah coming in the back door,* I decided. Groggy and disoriented from my afternoon nap, I dragged myself into a sitting position.

Hannah stuck her head through my bedroom doorway and asked, "We still going to the movies?" I nodded. "We should leave here in about a half hour," she continued, "and from the looks of things you've got some work to do."

I heard her go downstairs and into the kitchen. Hannah Lopez and I had grown up together—her family lived two streets over. Her father had taught Bible study for years, and her mother had introduced me to the best Mexican food I had ever eaten. The thought of her tamales made my mouth water.

I walked over to my full-length mirror. Hannah was right—I looked terrible. My long auburn hair was matted from sweat, and my black-smudged eyes stood out in my pale face. Everyone else in my family had dark hair and an olive complexion, so when I was born a fair redhead, it was a bit of a surprise. My mom claimed I took after my great-grandmother, Eleanor Langston, a fiery Scottish woman with red hair, but my brothers ignored this and tried for years to convince me I was adopted. Then one Sunday before church, old Gus Barney, known for his odd behavior, loudly asked my mom if our mailman had red hair. My mom rolled her eyes and shushed him, but my precocious ten-year-old self kicked him in the shins just as hard as I could with my new Payless wedges. Once apologies were exchanged and our family was settled into a church pew, my mom whispered to me that Mr. Barney wasn't in his right mind.

Remembering that story made me chuckle. After repairing my makeup and throwing my hair into a bun, I went downstairs to the kitchen. Hannah was just finishing half of a homemade burrito. She handed me the other half. "Long night of studying?" she asked.

I nodded as I took a bite.

"I hear that," she said. "I spent a good portion of the night writing a paper exploring what Charlotte Brontë might have been thinking when she wrote *Jane Eyre*— politically motivated statement against child abuse, or a new take on romance? I went with the political perspective. It will get me a better grade."

I laughed around another bite of burrito. In so many ways Hannah and I were like twins: outspoken, opinionated, not afraid to take risks. But when it came to our career paths, we couldn't have been more different. She loved the fluid, relative world of literature, while I was a math major. I liked things to add up to one right answer. We had planned on rooming together, but my decision to housesit for my parents changed that. Hannah lived near campus, not wanting to drive back and forth every day, but she still slept over at my parents' house from time to time. Of course, when our class schedule allowed, we hung out at school.

"Anyone new coming tonight?" I asked. We were going to see the new Jack Ryan movie with some friends from her on-campus Christian youth group. Both Hannah and I had dated here and there, but nothing serious, and the dating landscape had faded somewhat in the past few months. Although there were plenty of available guys with all kinds of values, Hannah and I both held to the Christian standards we had been raised with, even if it meant more than a few dateless weekends.

"Not that I know of," she replied. "But I'm with you. A few new faces would be nice."

We went back upstairs and brushed our teeth, and I put on some lip gloss. Looking in the mirror at both of us made me smile. With her short, raven-black hair and olive skin, she looked more like my family than I did.

The movie was good, enhanced by Chris Pine's radiantly blue eyes and the creepiness of Kenneth Branagh's character. The good guy won, the bad guy lost. It all added up just the way I liked it. Sadly, though, no new young men showed up with our singles group.

When I got home, I checked my obituary email and found a new message from Stella Perkins, with the subject line "Ollie and his tractor." My hand almost shook as I opened the email.

Ollie should have died on his tractor, but he didn't. Heaven knows he loved the thing enough— I'm surprised he didn't try to take it with him. I know you explain how people die, and it bothers me that I can't say more. It's all on the up-and-up. It just didn't happen on the tractor.

I got my cell phone out and called Mr. Jonas.

Garland "Gus" Barney
1917–2011

Garland Barney died at the age of ninety-four from a broken neck, the result of a fall while in a fit of the shakes. He was called Gus by those who loved him, and known as Grandpa Gus by his grandson David, who emailed me with the interesting information from which this obituary was compiled.

The last decade of Gus's life was awful; he suffered from more ailments and disorders than anyone could count, everything from gout to phlebitis. Yet David wants to set the record straight, claiming that what appeared to be a trial by fire was actually the happiest time of his grandpa's life . . . and it was all David's fault.

At the age of eighty-four, Grandpa Gus received a computer as a birthday gift, but had no idea what it could do until David introduced him to the internet. Gus chanced upon the WebMD site and discovered the names and symptoms of all kinds of disorders. The wheels in his old mind began to turn, and he devised a plan that enabled him to get away with the two things he loved to do most: behave badly and annoy his wife.

He was immediately struck with strange sleep disorders, causing him to have crazy sleep patterns, but which really allowed him to lie in bed all day sneak-reading Louis L'Amour novels, and to stay up all night playing online video games, another thing he discovered on his computer. One time he came down with a hideous case of carbuncles, a delicate crafting of tapioca pudding and red play dough. His wife was so repulsed she stayed with her sister for two weeks, giving Gus the chance to binge-watch the complete Lonesome Dove *series. Discovering the world of dementia and Alzheimer's was for Gus a virtual treasure trove. Having been a rancher his whole life, he had quite the collection of cowboy paraphernalia, which he often used in his dementia-induced charades. One of the more memorable antics was when he strode into his wife's quilting bee wearing nothing but boots, spurs, and a neckerchief and proceeded to rope all the ladies, pretending they were cows.*

Gus was known to let loose with a swear word here and there, something that particularly distressed his wife. But when he suddenly came down with Tourette syndrome, he began to swear like a sailor, along with twitching and barking like a dog. This particular syndrome always seemed to be at its worst during church. Parkinson's allowed him to shake so badly that he broke all of his wife's large collection of Precious Moments figurines, something David didn't mind so much because he thought they were weird. Sadly, it was this elaborate shaking that caused Gus's fatal fall. He was going for the last Precious Moments figurine—the one of a small boy in a cowboy hat and diaper trying to rope a kitten—that was hidden high in the back of the top cabinet shelf. Gus stood on a kitchen chair and had nearly snagged the figurine when his wife unexpectedly walked into the room. Gus feigned a shaking spell, lost his balance, and fell, snapping his neck on their antique buffet.

David wants to thank all those who served and put up with Grandpa Gus during these trying years. Many people felt genuine compassion for Gus and gave countless hours of service in the form of yard work, errands, and meals. "All I can do now is apologize for his behavior. Every time I tried exposing him, he'd do something awful like creating an extremely unflattering dating profile for me on Tinder or hacking into my Facebook account and announcing to the world that I was quarantined with MRSA. I had created a monster!"

David found some comfort in the fact that his grandpa died doing what he loved and that he had succeeded in breaking the last figurine. David would also like everyone to know that his grandma sold the ranch and bought a beach-front condo in Aruba, where she currently lives. Contact David for her address if you'd like to write.

Five

I called Mr. Jonas and told him about the two emails. "Oliver Moore died a few months ago, right?" he asked.

"Yep."

"Stella Perkins's husband, Art, repairs tractors, right?"

"Yep," I said.

"And Betty's one of those . . . interesting hat ladies?"

"Yep."

"Do you think Oliver and Betty were . . .?" My boss's voice trailed off.

"I don't know," I replied. Mr. Jonas and I decided to talk in person the next day, and he planned to invite his friend's son, Jackson Clark, to join us. Jackson was a detective with the Missoula Police Department, under Sergeant Ezekiel "Ez" Perdue, a man known for his unorthodox methods of enforcing the law. Mr. Jonas had saved Ez's life more than once when they served together in Vietnam.

We met at a chain restaurant I'd describe as a serious dive. I hate the place but picked it because none of my university friends ate there, so there was very little chance I would be spotted by someone I knew. I didn't want anyone to see me with the guy who ran the newspaper and suspect me of being the secret obituary writer.

While Mr. Jonas and I waited for Jackson, we tried to figure out a connection between Betty Whipple, Stella Perkins, and Oliver Moore. After a few minutes my boss said, "There is Jackson," and slid out of the booth to stand.

My back was to the door, so I twisted around. I don't know what I expected, but it wasn't this. The guy walking toward us was tall and muscular—athletic, even—and he moved with purpose. Wearing a black suit with a crisp white button-down shirt, he appeared to be in his late twenties. Short brown hair framed his ruggedly handsome face, and as he came closer I noticed his strikingly blue eyes. Then he flashed a smile—with dimples. After stifling a sigh, I made a mental note to quit watching all those crime dramas where the detectives look grimy and tired.

Mr. Jonas hugged him as if he were family and then turned to me. "Jackson, this is Lizzy—Elizabeth Langston. Lizzy, this is Jackson Clark, a dear friend's son."

Smiling, Jackson took my hand in a firm handshake. I muttered a hello, still stunned by his dimples. Obviously noticing my nervousness, Mr. Jonas got that look in his eye—the same "you're a perfect match" expression he had when he introduced me to his nephew. But thankfully, this was no Leonard.

Mr. Jonas stepped aside and let Jackson slide into the booth. My boss got in next to him, so both men were facing me across the table. Just as Mr. Jonas started to say something, a server appeared and asked for our order.

It was midmorning and I didn't feel hungry, so I said, "I'll just have a Diet Pepsi with lemon."

The server wrote it down and looked at Jackson, who smiled and declared, "I'll have the same."

I couldn't help but grin. *He's got looks* and *taste.*

"You two aren't hungry?" Mr. Jonas said. "I'm buying."

Jackson and I shook our heads. Then we chuckled as Mr. Jonas ordered half of the left side of the menu for himself. With one eyebrow arched, the server wrote it all down, then hurried away. As long as I'd known Mr. Jonas, he'd eaten like a linebacker but remained thin and wiry.

"Lizzy, I grew up with Jackson's dad, John, a great guy. Your mom and dad are getting ready to go to Africa, right?" Mr. Jonas gave the back of Jackson's neck a squeeze.

"Yes, that's right. They take our church's youth group on a humanitarian mission every summer," Jackson answered with pride.

"Well, isn't that great," Mr. Jonas said just before he turned his matchmaking agenda smile on me. He knew about my dating standard—that I wouldn't date someone who didn't hold to Christian values. My gaze narrowed a little toward my boss, but I took the bait.

"Yeah, that's great," I agreed. "Jackson, did you ever go on one of their humanitarian trips?"

"He did. Where was it you went?" Mr. Jonas put in.

Jackson flashed him a you-know-where-it-was look, then politely masked it and glanced at me. "I went with them to New Zealand once."

"New Zealand? Wow," I responded.

"What a great place to go, huh?" chimed Mr. Jonas. "Beautiful pictures. Right out of *The Lord of the Rings.*

You should have seen Jackson when he got home. Did the Maori *haka* dance. Painted his chest and everything."

Jackson gave Mr. Jonas an incredulous look.

"Really? Are there pictures of that?" I teased.

Laughing, Jackson nodded and then turned to Mr. Jonas. "I could have you arrested for this level of embarrassment. Maybe I need to call my mom's friend Leslie and see if she'd like a blind date with a newspaper publisher." My mouth flew open as I looked from Jackson to Mr. Jonas.

"Oh, we've been trying to fix Mr. Jonas up for quite some time," Jackson explained. "It never seems to work out, though, does it?"

Mr. Jonas responded with a stern stare.

"I have too," I said, "but I've given him a break since we came to an understanding. But all bets might be off now." I smiled knowingly at Mr. Jonas.

The server brought our drinks and said she'd be back in a minute with the food. Mr. Jonas took a few gulps of his water, then asked, "So, Jackson, what do you think of these emails?"

I grinned at the abrupt change of subject. Jackson took a small notepad and pen out of his coat pocket and was beginning to say something when the server returned with Mr. Jonas's brunch. It took him half a minute to organize his plates, but then he started to eat and motioned for Jackson to continue.

"I've heard of these obituaries," Jackson said. "So you're the secret writer?"

I nodded uneasily. Until that moment, only my parents and Mr. Jonas knew I wrote the secret obituaries.

Jackson reached over and patted my hand. "Don't worry. Your secret's safe with me." My skin tingled at his touch, and his blue eyes calmed me a little.

I glanced at Mr. Jonas, who was smiling in triumph, his cheeks full of pancakes and fried eggs. He quickly swallowed and said, "I told Jackson about the emails when we spoke on the phone. We can trust him, and trust his advice. Not only is he a dear friend's son, but he works for Ez."

Although Mr. Jonas hadn't told me much about his time in Vietnam, he had mentioned his close friendship with Sergeant Perdue, and the reason for it.

I shifted my gaze back to Jackson, who said, "Since Mr. Moore wasn't ill or under a doctor's care, an autopsy was performed. I looked at the report. The medical examiner found no signs of foul play. Mr. Moore died of natural causes—a heart attack, to be more specific. It turns out his heart was damaged, probably from childhood rheumatic fever. The guy went his whole life with a bad heart and probably didn't even know it."

I exhaled a breath and took a sip of my soda. Mr. Jonas stopped eating long enough to seem relieved.

"These emails are curious, but we don't have any evidence to go on," Jackson went on. "I could question these women, but I don't want to scare them off. More importantly, I don't want to break the trust they have in Cutlip's secret obituary writer. I'd rather wait and see if they give you any more information. Or maybe someone else will come forward."

The detective's line of reasoning made sense. Mr. Jonas signaled his agreement while wiping egg yolk from the corner of his mouth. Then he said, "I don't want to break any laws, but Lizzy and these obituaries are the reason my delivery business still exists. I can't afford to lose it."

"I understand," Jackson replied. "Lizzy, if it's all right with you, let's stay in close contact. If you receive more emails about Mr. Moore's death, please forward them to me, and we'll see where this goes. Who knows? Maybe you'll have the makings of a great story."

Jackson glanced from Mr. Jonas to me. I voiced my agreement, while my boss grinned like a Cheshire cat. Of course he liked the idea of a story that would sell a lot of newspapers, but he also clearly enjoyed playing matchmaker.

Jackson cleared his throat. "I've only been to Cutlip a few times and mainly just drove through town. It's an interesting name. Who came up with that?"

"It was named after Silas Cutlip, the first settler in this area," Mr. Jonas said. "Supposedly he was a grouchy old farmer with only one leg—lost the other one in the Civil War. His youngest daughter, Sophronia Cutlip, lived to be 105. She died a few years ago. Lizzy did her obituary. Sophronia was a very opinionated woman." Mr. Jonas scraped each of his plates.

Jackson looked to me as if wanting confirmation. "Apparently she felt the need to set the world straight before she left it," I said. "She was pretty complicated."

Jackson and I exchanged contact information while Mr. Jonas stacked his empty plates and handed them to the server in exchange for the bill. As Jackson typed my number into his phone, I wondered how old he was. I was definitely attracted to him and looking forward to our "staying in close contact," whatever that turned out to be. On that note, he handed me his business card with his information on it. I slipped the card into my wallet.

As we walked out of the restaurant, I wondered what kind of car a detective would drive. I had brought my parents' Tahoe that day, since they'd asked me to drive it a few times a week to keep things working. My trusty Impala was back at the house. Of course, Mr. Jonas had driven his old white Chevy truck, a workhorse of a machine that he had owned for as long as I'd worked for him.

"Thanks for coming, Jackson," Mr. Jonas said as they embraced in the parking lot.

"Not a problem," Jackson replied, giving Mr. Jonas's back a thump. He turned to me and extended his hand. "Nice to meet you, Lizzy. I'll call you later, and don't forget to forward those emails to me."

"Definitely," I said, impressed by his thoroughness and attention to detail. He said goodbye to both of us and headed toward a dark sedan.

Mr. Jonas's eyes bored into mine with anticipation. "So what'd you think of him?"

I smirked. "How about I suggest you as a speaker at the next single mingle for ages 46 and up? No doubt they would be fascinated to learn all about the exciting world of newspaper publishing."

At my boss's disappointed look, I relented. "He seems very nice. How old is he?"

"You can ask him when he calls you later. Jackson's the real deal, Lizzy Girl. They don't make 'em better than him. So be nice, okay?"

I laughed and headed for the Tahoe.

Sophronia Cutlip
1904–2009

Sophronia Cutlip died of a brain aneurysm at the age of 105. She was the youngest daughter of town-founder Silas Cutlip, who lived to the age of ninety-nine, providing Sophronia with fifty-nine years of stern instruction regarding how "his" town should look. In fact, his dying wish was for Sophronia to spend the rest of her years ensuring that the people of Cutlip upheld his legacy.

Driven to uphold her father's request, Sophronia pounded the sidewalks in her sensible day heels, visiting homes and businesses. She carried a clipboard with a list of Cutlip's statutes regarding the maintenance of private yards, porches, and house fronts, as well as a list of various laws pertaining to business signage and the like. Infractions were immediately noted and reported. As the years passed, the task took its toll on Sophronia's health and finances, even though she did finally convince Phil, the manager at Walgreens, to give her a discount on "those pricy Dr. Scholl's inserts" in exchange for some "moral instruction on his cosmetic displays." Exhausted and suffering with bunions, Sophronia feared she would let her father down—until the glorious day she discovered email.

Most days the good people of Cutlip woke to an instructional email from Sophronia in their inboxes. In one of her last messages, she asked me to "send just one more email from the Great Beyond" to emphasize the things she considered most pertinent.

Personal appearance was of the utmost importance to Sophronia. How one dressed reflected the community one was raised in. Yoga pants should be worn only for the actual doing of yoga, preferably in the privacy of one's own home. Flip-flops are annoying and usually reveal unkempt toes. And the wearing of tank tops, particularly by elderly men, should be banned. "The upper torso of a man 'cashes out' by age thirty and therefore should be covered." Sophronia quit shopping at Walmart because, as she said it, "the lack of dress standards caused me to have heart palpitations."

Unkempt lawns were a particular offense to Sophronia, who claimed that "lawns give the town's first impression, and residents who desecrate their yards with tacky windmills, clay donkeys, and garden gnomes—and you know who you are—should remove them immediately." Sophronia blames the migraine headaches that plagued her the last ten years of her life on "Bonnie Swoape's stubborn use of toilets and bathtubs as flower planters."

Sophronia was married to Richmond Haynie, who, after months of attempted courtship, finally "got it right" by showing up at her front door with pink snapdragons, The Best of Barry Manilow *on CD, and a heavy dose of Old Spice. The marriage was over when one Saturday morning Richmond, clad in cargo shorts, a Hawaiian-print shirt, and flip-flops, announced that he and Sophronia were going to the swap meet to buy lawn ornaments. It was a no-*

contest divorce, though Richmond made "quite the show of his stress-induced rash and hair loss."

Sophronia described cell phones as "rude and ridiculous," declared that texting should be outlawed. If someone texted you, how could you tell if he or she were "dressed appropriately with fresh-smelling breath and no bed head"— all requisites to having a conversation with Sophronia. She loved her television and was partial to crime dramas and Jeopardy. She thought Alex Trebek should dye his hair, Jason Bourne would make an excellent president, and all Kardashians should be deeply ashamed of themselves.

Sophronia knows the citizens of Cutlip will miss her daily instructions, and so that they do not wander misguided, she magnanimously saved all her emails on ten flash drives for ready-reference. These flash drives are held in safekeeping by Ned Wheeler the mortician—who, according to Sophronia, needs to "buy a new suit, wax his knuckles, and visit a dentist."

Six

After class, I did a long shift at the tutor lab. I loved working with high school kids and received some of my best obituary feedback and carrier gossip while helping students solve for X.

At home, I checked my obituary email. Nothing new. I forwarded Betty's and Stella's messages to the email address on Jackson Clark's business card. I plowed through a few pages of homework problems and then had to rest my eyes.

An hour later I woke when my phone chimed loudly. Sure enough, I had two new emails—one from Doris Peet and one from Madge Abernathy. I opened the messages and forwarded them to Jackson without reading them. To give him time to receive the emails, I ate a quick snack before dialing his number. He answered on the second ring.

"You looking at your email?" I asked.

"Yeah. I just saw the ones you sent," he replied. "Have you read them?"

"I'm about to." I read Doris's first, silently.

I can't stop crying! The sight of Ollie dead and lifeless keeps haunting me. It has to be a punishment from God. We didn't think before we did what we did, and now I realize it was wrong. Since you won't tell anyone, maybe confiding in you will settle my delicate nerves.

I knew Mrs. Peet and her "delicate nerves." Rarely did she speak three sentences without crying. Her lengthy, weepy comments in Bible study were legendary.

"Okay, I just read Doris's message," I told Jackson. "She mentioned 'we,' so it sounds like the three women were together when they saw Oliver dead. But apparently not near his tractor."

"That's what I've gathered, too," Jackson said.

I double-clicked on Madge Abernathy's message.

I feel it only appropriate that I share this information with someone. Because of your anonymity, you were the obvious choice. Oliver Moore was nowhere near his tractor when he passed on, though for him that would have been a proper setting. Sadly, his was a less-than-dignified passing.

"I wonder what she means by 'less-than-dignified,'" I commented. All I knew about Mrs. Abernathy was that she and her husband were very wealthy.

"No clue," Jackson said. "But I have an idea. You know the town and these women. What if we follow them to see if their paths cross—see what they can tell us without knowing we're watching? We can use my car, which has tinted windows."

The plan made sense, but I knew he didn't need me to help carry it out. As a police detective, he could find out where these women lived. But I liked the idea of spending a few hours with him and his dimples, so I agreed. The next day was Saturday, and we decided to meet up in the Walmart parking lot.

Seven

The inside of Jackson's car looked like the outside—dark and clean and shiny, very detective-like. He wore jeans and a blue button-down shirt, which made his eyes appear even bluer, if that was possible. His light aftershave made me think of the ocean.

I had given my appearance a little more thought than normal for a Saturday morning. After fifteen minutes in front of my closet I'd finally decided on jeans, a white blouse, and sandals—my default outfit when I don't know what to wear. My hair is usually leftovers from Friday night thrown in a ponytail. But I washed and curled it that Saturday morning and left it down and loose.

The effort paid off. As Jackson opened the car door for me, he said, "Good morning. You look beautiful." I smiled and slipped into the vehicle.

I'd made a list of the four women's addresses and marked their homes on a map. This was completely redundant for a detective, since he could find the addresses in the police database and then GPS them in his car, but I wanted him to know I was thorough and detailed.

He took the map and looked at it. "Which one do you think we should start with?" He glanced up and smiled at me, and the sight of his dimples made my breath catch.

He handed the map back to me, and I pretended to study while I gathered my thoughts. "We're not far from Doris Peet's home, so we could start with her," I said finally. "She retired from nursing, but I think she still picks a shift up here and there. She also volunteers a few days a week at a homeless shelter in the city."

"Sounds good to me." Jackson pulled out of the parking lot and headed toward Doris's street. Since Jackson didn't look at my map again, I slid it between the console and my seat. Maybe he had the addresses committed to his detective memory. "So, how well do you know Doris?" he asked.

"She goes to Bible study. Anyone who has heard her comments knows all about her life." I smiled.

Jackson laughed. "One of those, huh?"

"Yep. I'll give you the highlights. She's been divorced for several years, her children are grown and don't appreciate her, she prays daily that her ex-husband will have the strength to repent of his many sins, and the only ones who really understand her are her cats. And she cries—a lot."

"Wow," Jackson sighed, and we both chuckled.

"She does give a lot of service in the church and community," I added. "It's just hard to be around someone who cries about everything."

"Well, let's see what Mrs. Peet has to show us," Jackson said. He parked a few houses down, giving us a discreet yet clear view of her home.

He undid his seat belt and moved his seat back a little, so I did the same with mine. Then I panicked a little, realizing we might be there for several hours. Usually I had no problem holding my own in a conversation with peers, but Jackson was older and professional and very attractive. *Oh no, I hope we don't run out of things to talk about.*

"So, tell me about your school," Jackson began. "Mr. Jonas tells me you're a math major. I hate math."

I laughed at Jackson's grimace and told him about how much I loved math and teaching, and how my goal was to conquer math-hate one student at a time. Jackson said he had originally majored in international finance but switched to criminal justice. After graduation he went through the police academy. He had made detective a few years ago.

"How old are you, anyway?" I said.

Jackson glanced sideways at me. "I just turned thirty last month, and I bet I've been on way more blind dates than you."

"Oh, I've been on plenty. Have you met Mr. Jonas's nephew Leonard?"

"The one with the lazy eye?"

"Yeah, that's him."

"Well, I don't envy his vision problem, but socially he seems a little off," Jackson replied. "I'd say one evening with him should count for at least two or three dates. Then again, I don't really know him, so he might be the nicest guy in the world."

"Yeah, he might," I said, then changed the subject. "Tell me about your parents. I bet they are excited to go to Africa."

Jackson spoke about his parents, then said he had three younger sisters who were married with children. When he began telling me about his nieces and nephews, I knew I wouldn't need to ask another question for a long time.

A few minutes later, though, an old sedan pulled into Mrs. Peet's drive. It had once been blue but had faded to a tired gray, the sides and bumper rusted by too many Montana winters. Doris got out, dressed in dirty, crumpled medical scrubs. She looked tired, as if she had worked all night. She walked to her front door and unlocked it. What happened next should have been videoed. A wave of cats poured out the door. They went everywhere, making a break for freedom. Doris scrambled to gather all the screeching, hissing felines and force them back inside her home.

"Didn't she say the only ones who understand her are her cats?" Jackson asked.

"That is correct, yes," I said, shaking my head in amazement at the scene.

"That's sad."

We waited for a little while to see if Doris would leave. After about thirty minutes of no action, we decided to try Betty Whipple's home a few streets over. As we drove I told Jackson what I knew about Mrs. Whipple.

"The Red Hat Society? That's for older women, right? Usually single?" he asked. "Sometimes they act kind of boisterous at restaurants?"

"Yes. The best way to describe Betty's personality is to say she fits well into that group."

Jackson frowned, looking puzzled. "Assuming these emails are connected, how could two women as different as Mrs. Peet and Mrs. Whipple cross paths?"

"No clue," I responded, having mulled that over many times myself.

We parked across the street but down one house, giving us a good view of Betty Whipple's brightly painted Victorian with a manicured lawn and an abundance of garden gnomes. Jackson's eyes grew large as he took it all in. After a few minutes of comfortable silence, he asked, "Is Mrs. Whipple a member of the Community Church?"

"Yes," I replied. "We don't always see her at Sunday meetings, but I hear she has been involved with the single mingles."

Suddenly, Betty's front door opened and she emerged, wearing a form-fitting outfit made of bright-pink leopard-print fabric, probably Spandex. One of her hands grasped the handles of a large pink tote, while the other hand cradled a small dog.

"There she is," I exclaimed. "That's Betty."

She backed her vehicle out of the driveway and drove down the road. When she reached the end of the street and turned, Jackson started his car. "There's kind of a psychology to following someone," he told me. "When most people drive, they are only aware of a certain space around them. Imagine a circumference of awareness around Mrs. Whipple. We stay just outside that circle, but close enough to see her, and we're good. Enter too many times into a driver's awareness, and even the most distracted one will be spooked. At this point, Betty Whipple seems pretty distracted."

I had to agree. She was driving all over the place, and though we were too far back to see, I imagined her playing with her dog and fixing her hair in the mirror on her visor. We followed her to a dog groomer, Canine Cuteness, where she dropped off her dog. Then Betty walked two doors down to Haute Nails, a nail salon.

"So how are your nails looking today?" Jackson asked as he reached over and picked up my hand. "Should I send you in for a manicure and a chat with Mrs. Whipple?" His strong, warm touch made me quiver inside.

"These nails probably need some attention," I said a bit breathlessly.

Jackson squeezed my hand before letting go, but rested his arm next to mine on the console. "We won't blow our cover just yet," he said.

Good, I thought. It felt so comfortable yet exciting to sit quietly, arms touching, and I was no longer anxious about the hours ahead. We talked a little here and there, about silly things, like the cost of having a dog groomed, and why women paint crazy designs on their nails.

Eventually Mrs. Whipple emerged from the salon and went to pick up her dog. Minutes later she got back in her car, taking extra care with her nails as she settled the dog and started the engine. She headed toward the city. We discreetly followed her for several miles before I wondered aloud where she was going.

"It's lunchtime, so my guess is she's meeting friends at a restaurant," Jackson replied. "I don't know about you, but I could eat. Let's hope she picks a good place."

"So, how old are you?" he asked all of a sudden.

"Twenty. I turn twenty-one in a few months."

"I already knew that. I just wanted to give you the chance to tell me I'm too old for you."

"Mr. Jonas said you're very immature, so I figure that nine-year gap is more like three or four," I teased.

"I knew my immaturity would pay off someday. And Mr. Jonas told me you were wise beyond your years, so this is kind of awkward, but you're a bit old for me."

I narrowed my gaze at Jackson and grinned. "I can't imagine him saying anything close to that, but if you asked me out, I wouldn't say no."

"Good, because I'm about to buy you lunch at Mimi's Café." I hadn't noticed, but we had followed Mrs. Whipple to the mall. Several restaurants surrounded it, and sure enough she had pulled up at Mimi's.

"We can't go into the same restaurant, can we?" I asked, wondering about the circumference-of-awareness thing.

"Not just yet, but it's a nice day and she's carrying her puppy in her purse, so I'm thinking she'll be seated on the patio, where they allow that sort of thing. If so, we'll get a table inside. The windows are tinted so we will see her, but she won't see us."

"Ah, smart. But what if she sits inside?" I said.

"Then we drive through that Carl's Jr. and eat in the car while we wait for her, and we hope she walks out with the person or people she's having lunch with. But we won't have to, because look who's taking advantage of the lovely weather." Jackson pointed to Mrs. Whipple and her puppy, who were being seated at a patio table.

Eight

Jackson picked out a table inside Mimi's where we could see Betty Whipple through a window. Fortunately, the hostess allowed us to sit there. Three women I didn't recognize showed up at Betty's table, all dressed extravagantly and carrying small, well-groomed dogs in dog totes. Jackson and I watched the ladies chat while I ate an Oriental salad and he devoured a French-dip sandwich. When the women seemed almost ready to leave, Jackson quickly paid our bill and we headed to the car. There was no need to hurry, though, because the women must've spent several minutes hugging and saying goodbye—and kissing each other's dogs—before leaving.

Jackson and I followed Betty to her house. Once she went inside, we parked a few houses away on her side of the road. We thought perhaps she was dropping off the dog and going somewhere else, but after an hour, we decided she was probably in for the day. Jackson started the car and we headed over to Madge Abernathy's home.

As we turned onto their street, I said, "The Abernathys are quite well off. Madge's husband is an orthodontist."

"Good to know." Jackson paused as if in thought. "Those women are an interesting bunch. Too bad we couldn't hear what they were saying at the restaurant. Maybe we'd already know what they did to poor Oliver Moore."

I chuckled at the idea of Mr. Moore plunked in the middle of such an odd mixture of women. "What if we are going at this the wrong way?" I asked suddenly. "What if we should be looking at his life?"

"I wondered that too, so I did a thorough background check. There was nothing that would seem to connect him to any of these women, except for their attendance at the Cutlip Community Church." Jackson stopped the car at the curb. The Abernathy house was barely visible around a curve. He studied the area for a minute, then said, "There seems to be more traffic than usual on a street like this. Let's wait and see what's going on."

I had noticed more cars than usual, but after half an hour it became clear that something was happening at the Abernathy home. Jackson positioned his car where we could see everyone more clearly. About twenty older couples arrived for what appeared to be a backyard barbecue. Though I recognized some of the party guests, our email ladies were not among them.

"How about we call it a day and go get some ice cream or something?" Jackson asked me after a while.

"Sounds great," I replied. He gave me a look that made my stomach flutter. We had spent the day together, and I didn't want it to end. I'd never felt this way about a guy—it was good but scary. *Is scary-good a word?* I wondered.

Soon we arrived at my favorite ice cream place, Sweet Nothings. Jackson ordered chocolate fudge, and I got my usual praline pecan. We sat on the porch enjoying the heavenly dessert and the sultry evening.

We ate in silence until he said, "Tell me more about the obituaries you write. I think they're ingenious."

I grinned. "Thanks. Did Mr. Jonas tell you how the whole thing got started?"

"Not really."

I explained everything, and Jackson listened intently. Then he asked, "When you get a request and information, is it from family, friends, or someone who knows he or she is close to the end?"

"It can be any or all of those, and each case is unique," I said. "I try to spend time putting it all together to create something the deceased person would be happy with. This may sound silly, but I actually pray about what to include. If someone asks for my services, it's because they or a close friend or relative feel they haven't been understood. I take that seriously." I met Jackson's eyes and watched his mouth slowly form a smile. Something inside me shifted pleasantly.

"So tell me about some of these people who you've helped. Who has been your favorite?"

I scraped the bottom of my cup—I was a fast ice-cream eater and didn't usually get a brain freeze. Jackson was only halfway through his ice cream. I set my cup and spoon on our table and folded my arms, thinking. Finally, I answered, "Well, it's hard to pick a favorite, but I could tell you about some of the more interesting ones." I got my phone out and pulled up my obituary file.

Mavis Nettles
1918–2010

Mavis Nettles died of a heart attack at the age of ninety-two. According to her sisters, Melba and Martha, she passed on "because she decided she wanted to." Reportedly, Mavis controlled her final departure just like she controlled everything else in her life. Her sisters emailed me and requested this obituary to "set some things straight."

Melba and Martha described Mavis as spoiled, brattish, and prone to tantrums her entire life. She was the favorite of her parents and, therefore, "was able to do as she pleased," despite her siblings' outrage. She never did her chores, her homework, or her hair, and if challenged on any of these points, she would slap and bite. Her sisters declared that Mavis would "give our favorite clothes to charity, tell our friends we had lice, and shave our dolls bald." Mavis would write "untoward love letters and sign our names, then send them to the meanest and oddest boys in school." Martha was a particular target for this, claiming, "I don't know what she wrote, but it took me a good six months to get rid of that awful Dean Bottoms!" Apparently Mavis was the reason neither Melba nor Martha married, because "no man could handle that for a sister-in-law." Mavis's parents remained blind to Melba and Martha's plight, claiming these two sisters "had it coming."

According to her sisters, Mavis was unworthy of any kind of acknowledgment from her parents, yet she received what was considered the "family treasure," the much-longed-for opal brooch of Great-Grandmother Nettles. Both Melba and Martha felt this ballyhooed brooch should have adorned their chests rather than being "pinned over such a hateful heart" as their sister's. "So what?" Melba and Martha said in regards to Mavis's career as a hospice nurse and 9-1-1 dispatcher, and her subsequent three missions to Calcutta to work with Mother Teresa in the leper colonies. It was all a "ruse for the brooch," Mavis's sisters claimed. Melba and Martha spent a good portion of their lives looking for this brooch, but Mavis hid it well. Her sisters never found it, and in the end Melba theorized that Mavis "gave it to that Teresa woman, in India."

I received one email from Mavis, one week prior to her death. I'll quote it verbatim:

"You know Ned Wheeler, the mortician? So do I. The brooch is in my pocket. Come and get it."

Jackson shook his head, chuckling. "So once you published the obituary, did the sisters dig up Mavis's grave to recover the brooch?"

I shook my head, chuckling. "Not as far as I know. The sisters must've decided getting the family heirloom wasn't worth jail time. But some kids watched the graveyard like hawks. It about drove Ned crazy. Not only is he the town mortician, but he also looks after the graveyard. He was picking up candy wrappers and pop cans for days."

"Do you know the sisters? Are they really as awful as they seem?" asked Jackson.

"From what I knew of Mavis, she was a kind and caring person. I never met her sisters—they don't live around here. But if their emails are any indication, they were something else. It's interesting that Melba and Martha wanted to get even with Mavis, but what it really did was help everyone understand the type of family she came from. I was glad I could do that for Mavis."

"I won't ever complain about my sisters again." Jackson grinned, then said with a gleam in his eye, "Read me some more obituaries."

In the dimming light of near-dusk, Tito flipped on his pizzeria sign across the street from Sweet Nothings. "Okay," I told Jackson. I flipped through a few more obits on my phone. "This is a good one."

Harlan Leach
1961–2009

Harlan Leach, co-owner of Leach Pest Control, died a sudden and unsavory death at the age of forty-eight. He ate lunch every day at Tito Abbadellis' Pizzeria—the Leach and Abbadelli families being "good friends and all." One day after eating his favorite triple-meat calzone, Harlan headed out for an afternoon of bug spraying. Tito, a marketing-conscious entrepreneur, had upped the sidewalk sign-spinner craze a notch (and saved a buck at the same time) by using a well-endowed mannequin he chanced upon at Goodwill. He rigged up a small motor and a few screws and had a free sign spinner that whirled a sign around all day without whining about being laughed at by pedestrians or flipped off by passing motorists.

Sadly, on the ill-fated calzone-lunch day, something came unhinged on Tito's buxom sign spinner. Harlan had his windows down and was leaving the parking lot when the sign broke free and did the horrible damage that flying flat things can do. Harlan died instantly.

You would think a death of this kind would stun the people of Cutlip, and it did. But for the bug-conscious housewives, this ugly death was eclipsed by what Harlan's brother and business partner, Elmore, discovered in Harlan's basement. It is to quiet the frayed nerves of these loyal customers that Elmore has requested my services.

Exterminators play an interesting and delicate role in a community—one few really think about. But to the housewives of Cutlip it is ever-present, primarily because an exterminator sees every square inch of their homes on a regular basis. To put it simply, the sloppy want their secrets kept, and the tidy want to know who the sloppy are. The Leach brothers had seen the quick demise of extermination businesses whose owners talked, so both Harlan and Elmore kept their lips sealed about their customers' housekeeping habits. Yet Harlan, being divorced with no children, had little to fill his free time and had, therefore, secretly created an elaborate monthly charting system where he judged the cleanliness of the homes he sprayed. He obviously had spent many hours in his basement rating homes on a scale of 1 to 10, for the detailed charts lined all the available wall space. Word of this got out and sent Harlan's customers into a panic. It was also rumored that after seeing his brother's extensive chart-work, Elmore laughed so hard he had to be helped to his truck.

Elmore felt this obituary would be the quickest way to assure Leach Pest Control customers—all faithful Cutlip Currier *subscribers—that all is well. He promises to act as a human vault to keep their secrets safe, and customers' bugs will be killed on a regular basis. For safety's sake, Harlan's charts are being stored with Ned Wheeler, the town mortician.*

Much to Tito's relief, the Leach family begged the county attorney not to press charges, the Abbadelli and Leach families being "friends and such." Of course the Leaches were promised free pizza and calzones for life. Tito now advertises his pizzeria with a traditional standing board sign out front. He did add a string of battery-operated lights, which everyone agrees is very eye-catching.

Nine

Once Jackson stopped laughing, I told him, "You know, not all the obituaries are funny. Some people ask me to say what they were never able to say while they were alive. Or they write to me before the memories fade, so that when they do pass away, their story can be told." I looked down at the document on my phone. "Conrad Wright's and Obediath McGinnis's were two of the saddest I've written."

Conrad Wright
1925–2012

Conrad Wright died of lung cancer at the age of eighty-seven. He did many brave things in his life, such as fighting in World War II, building a successful plumbing company from the ground up, and holding his son as he died from leukemia. Conrad was the quiet ear for our grief, and the strong sure hand for our plumbing woes. But the one thing he lacked the courage to do was tell his wife Mary how he really felt about her. He's requested my services for this, and I will quote him directly:

"I'm not long for this life and can't leave without letting my Mary know how I feel about her. I always wanted to tell her in person, but every time I tried to put voice and breath to the words flooding my mind, I decided they wouldn't be enough. I wished I would have said them anyway and let her determine their worth. Now that I'm leaving for good, it's my last chance to tell her, and the whole world might as well hear it too.

I always wanted to be with Mary. As soon as I kissed her goodbye in the morning and walked out the door, I missed her. When she was near, everything felt right. Hearing her voice as I came home each evening made my heart skip a beat, every single time. That is such a big part of life, the hellos and goodbyes and the time in between, just being together. Mary made all those moments so happy for me. I hope she knew, even though I didn't have the courage to tell her.

Obediath McGinnis
1931–2010

Obediath McGinnis died at the age of seventy-nine from complications of dementia. He was a handyman by trade, and for over forty years he fixed everything that broke in our homes and businesses. Intelligent and well-read, he had a particular love of poetry. His favorites included the writings of Isaiah and the beautiful language of the Psalms.

Often while Obediath repaired something, he would treat his customers to a few verses of whatever he had been reading the night before.

In his last few years, dementia shrank Obediath's world to the confines of his home. The cruelty of the disease ravaged his rich inner life, and for the first time there were things he could not fix. Yet the creative part of his mind would drive him to strap on his tool belt, bound down his front steps, and try to fix anything that needed fixing. It is these moments his family has asked me to share. With the aid of Obediath's personal nurse, who wrote his words exactly and which I will quote verbatim, we will go on a few repair calls with Obediath.

"The toast was burnt every time. Down the beautiful white bread would go, and up it would come, black as death. Her toaster was broken. And so was her heart. Words would go in her mind—I'd see their beauty register across her eyes. But when they tried to enter her heart they would pop back up, black as her toast. I could fix her toaster; that was easy. I couldn't fix her heart, though.

"It was easy to fix a bicycle. I always did that for free. I loved to line up the chain, to see the spokes spin in their circular dance, the pedals doing their own spin, with no small tennis shoe to hold them flat. Children loved to watch me fix their bikes because some of them needed to be fixed the same way. I wish people knew how simple it is to fix a child. You can put everything in the right place with just a few kind words and a hug. Then

they spin with joy, just like a bike. I never accepted payment for repairing a bike.

"All it takes for everything to go dark is one wire burning out. There are wires in us, wires that keep us lit up. I know some of mine have gone out because there are thoughts and memories I can't reach. I can feel them, their bright edge almost breaking through. If only I could fix the wire that would bring the light back."

Though the moon had come out, the shadows blended into darkness, but it was light where Jackson and I sat on the porch of Sweet Nothings. After several seconds of silence, he said, "When I first heard of these obituaries, I thought it was just a way to keep Abe in business. But now I see it's so much more. You really help people. I'll do everything I can to keep your involvement a secret and help figure out what happened to Mr. Moore."

I smiled, reached across the table, and took hold of his fingers. He rested his other hand on mine. His warm, masculine touch almost made me gasp out loud. We sat quietly for a minute. Then, without a word, we both got up, threw our empty cups in the garbage can, and headed toward his car.

On the drive to Walmart, we made plans to surveil a few of the ladies on Monday and Tuesday evenings. Too soon, Jackson pulled up next to my car. He turned off his ignition and came around to let me out.

"This was the nicest stakeout I've ever been on," he said as I stepped onto the asphalt.

I laughed a little. "This is the *only* stakeout I've been on, but if this is what it's like, sign me up." I clicked the remote to unlock my car, and Jackson swung open my driver's side door.

"I liked being with you today, Lizzy. Can I call you tomorrow—see how you're doing?"

Trying to breathe normally, I climbed into my car. "Yes, call me anytime."

"Talk to you tomorrow, then." Jackson shut my car door and thumped the roof twice. He waited, leaning against his vehicle while I started mine and drove off.

Ten

"So he's a thirty-year-old detective, huh?" asked Hannah.

"Yeah." At her smile, I added, "I know—he isn't someone the typical college girl would consider dating."

"It's okay, you know. He sounds like he has his act together. Find out more about him. He's spent some years on the police force . . . gotta be some stories there."

While I longed to share my secret job with my best friend, I had promised Mr. Jonas to only discuss it with my parents. I'd told Hannah that my boss introduced me to Jackson, which was true, and that we had plans for Monday evening, which was true, though of course it wasn't a date.

"So, dimples, too?" she teased. I laughed and put my feet up on the porch rail. We'd attended church with her family and had lunch at their house, and now she and I were hanging out at my place.

"Yes, dimples and really blue eyes," I said, trying not to drool at the thought of Jackson's smile. "He's also very athletic looking, but I guess as a cop you have to stay in shape."

Hannah and I had stayed fit with high school sports, and now we both enjoyed hiking and yoga, which was a good thing because we also loved to eat. We'd just stuffed ourselves with her mom's amazing enchiladas, which was why neither of us wanted to move from the porch.

I sighed. "What's even nicer than Jackson's looks is that he is kind. He seems genuinely interested in getting to know me. He's pretty straightforward, and as far as I can tell, he isn't a player. I'll definitely give it a chance."

Hannah laughed, then kicked my feet off the rail. I almost fell out of my chair when I heard my phone notify me of a new email.

"Oooh," I said as I looked at the screen.

"Dimple man?" asked Hannah.

It was an obituary email, but I said, "Oh, I've got to call Jackson." I headed into the house, needing privacy.

"I need to go anyway." Hannah grabbed her keys and sunglasses and waved as she went down the front steps.

I moved to my computer and opened my email, then dialed Jackson's number.

"Hi," he said. "I was just going to call you."

"Another email came in, and the subject line mentions Oliver. I'm forwarding the message to you now. Hannah was here when I got it, so I haven't read it yet."

"Okay. I'm on my computer, signing into my email." Jackson paused. "It's gotta be rough keeping something like this from your best friend for so long." I had told him all about Hannah during one of our stakeouts.

"Well, it hasn't been easy. I hate not telling her, but I feel like this is for the greater good." The email opened up on my screen. It was from Geraldine Nesbitt.

"Okay, the message came through," Jackson told me. "I'm clicking on it now." He chuckled softly as I began to read out loud:

> *I was with Ollie Moore when he took his last breath. To see such a virile, well-toned body suddenly become lifeless was shocking—I had to tell someone! It was nothing like any of the Lifetime movies I've seen. One minute his muscular, glistening arms are moving, and the next minute they're not. I volunteered to change his clothes— someone had to.*

"What? Is she serious?" I said between giggles.

Jackson chuckled. "Who is Geraldine Nesbitt?"

"All I know is she is divorced and is probably in her mid-sixties. She was on my paper route and would suntan on her front lawn in a swimsuit no woman her age should be seen in. I think she works at the women's clothing store, Chico's, at the mall."

"Well, we've definitely made some headway with this one. Apparently these women changed Oliver Moore's clothes after he died." Jackson sounded incredulous.

"I . . . I guess," I stammered, trying to wrap my head around the image. "But why?"

"I have no idea, but I know who we'll be watching Monday night."

"Oh yeah." I told Jackson there were a few *Cutlip Currier* carriers in my math tutor lab, so I'd listen tomorrow for any pertinent info. After agreeing to meet in the Walmart parking lot at 5:00, we said goodbye.

Eleven

"So, how long has she been on your route?" Dave asked in an obvious attempt at a whisper.

"Just a couple of weeks. Jonas changed up my route. You know how he likes to mess with us," Jordan said.

Dave huffed. "Yeah. So have you seen anything?"

"Dude, way more than I wanted to."

I had just spent the better part of an hour explaining Dave's and Jordan's homework to them and helping them study for finals. They were newspaper carriers, and I knew Mr. Jonas sometimes switched up routes to mess with them. He usually did it during an obituary dry spell, when we were bored to tears. And although I felt partially responsible for and slightly bad about Jordan's plight, whatever it was, I hoped it somehow related to Oliver Moore's mysterious passing. Keeping quiet, I tried to look engrossed in my grading.

"Is it true she does yard work in her bathing suit?" Dave asked Jordan.

"Yeah, if that's what you call it. It's sick, man. She's got to be like eighty years old, so why is she even wearing a bikini? Plus who does yard work at 4:30 in the morning?"

The two teens shook their heads in disgust. Realizing I'd been looking at the same page for too long, I made some marks and turned to the next.

"Has she tried to talk to you?" Dave asked.

"Every morning," Jordan groaned. "What's with that? I'm barely awake. Why would I want to, like, chat with some old lady in a bikini?"

"Dude, that's serious. All I know is, don't ever go inside her house."

My ears perked up as I calmly lifted another page.

"Why?" Jordan actually sounded afraid.

"You haven't heard of the Nesbitt Love Pit?" Dave said.

They were both silent for a moment as I thought, *Holy cow, they must be talking about Geraldine Nesbitt!*

"She supposedly has some special romantic room in her basement," Dave went on. "The Love Pit."

Another silence.

"Has anyone ever seen the room?" Jordan asked.

"Dean Tolman snuck in her yard one night and looked in the basement window. There was weird Latin music playing really loud, and she was dancing around in some flowing costume thing. Dude, it's totally true—you've got to be careful."

"Maybe she just likes to dance . . . by herself . . . wearing costumes," Jordan said hesitantly.

"What? That's not normal! I tell ya, she lures young guys in there and they never come out. Maybe you can ask Jonas to switch you."

"I can't do that. Mrs. Nesbitt bought me a summer pass at WaterWorld and gives my mom gift certificates to that ladies store she works at, Chickies or Chucky's or something. My mom loves it. She bought a necklace that looks like it's made out of a chain-link fence."

Dave inhaled slowly through closed teeth. "You're stuck, dude. You better watch your back."

"Yeah, thanks a lot," Jordan said. The two teens worked in silence for a few more minutes and then left.

My mind reeled. *A love pit?* It was probably just the workings of a teenage mind run amok. But how were the other women involved with such a colorful character as Geraldine?

Tonight's stakeout with Jackson had just taken on a whole new meaning.

Twelve

"A love pit?" Jackson said through his laughter.

"Yeah, that's what the carriers called it—the Nesbitt Love Pit," I replied.

"When I was growing up we had a neighborhood legend about a crazy old guy who buried cats alive in his yard—but this is definitely up a notch."

"She gardens in her bathing suit, at the crack of dawn. You've got to admit that's weird," I said. "And the whole dancing-in-her-basement thing."

"Yep, that's weird if it's true, but leave it to a teenage boy's mind to turn that into a 'love pit,'" Jackson replied.

Geraldine Nesbitt lived in a nice area, having supposedly done well in her divorce settlement. Jackson parked his car where we had a decent view of Geraldine's spacious, Spanish-style home with perfectly manicured lawns, shrubbery, and flower beds.

A few minutes later, Jackson whistled low as a red Jaguar entered the circular driveway. "What did her ex do?"

"I think he was in real estate," I answered.

Wearing black leggings, black stilettos, and a zebra-print top that looked painted on, an older woman climbed out of the vehicle and walked to the front door. Several heavy silver chains hung around her neck, almost appearing to pull her off balance.

"This is good, though. She's just making a *pit* stop." Jackson glanced at me. We both laughed again.

"How do you know that?" I asked, wiping my eyes. Suddenly I realized the Jaguar sat directly in front of a three-car garage. "Ah, I see what you mean. If she were done for the day she would have parked the Jag inside."

Jackson tilted his head and smirked. "Something tells me she rarely spends her evenings home alone."

Sure enough, in a few minutes Geraldine emerged from the house. She wore the same top and leggings but had added a short red skirt and a red scarf. She got into her car and pulled out of her drive. We followed discreetly. The light faded and the street lights started clicking on as evening approached. Geraldine Nesbitt headed for the city, trailed by a detective and a secret obituary writer.

Jackson reached over and took my hand, weaving his fingers through mine. "I think we're in for a colorful evening, Lizzy. You up for this?"

He probably wanted to warn me about the type of life Geraldine might be leading. He must've seen just about everything in his line of work. "You mean this is going to be different than taking a dog to lunch with the ladies?"

He chuckled. "That's exactly what I mean."

"I'm up for it. I'm dying to figure out what happened to Oliver."

"I still don't think there's any foul play here, or you wouldn't be getting the emails," Jackson said. "The women just need to share what's bothering them, and they know they can trust you. Somehow, though, we have to draw a common thread between them. Like you, I have no idea what it might be." Almost under his breath, he added, "We won't even talk about how illegal it is to disturb a corpse."

We followed Geraldine to a bar called Nona's Nugget. A large, sliding-glass wall was open, revealing a chic outdoor bar and dining area done in shades of gold. Jackson parked where we could see what was happening without it being obvious we were watching. I exhaled a sigh of relief.

Jackson squeezed my hand. "Don't worry, I'd never take you into a place like this. Though I'd brave it myself." He gave me a crooked smile.

"Thanks. But maybe I would be just as concerned if *you* went into a place like this. A few of those ladies look pretty aggressive." Several older women were seated, some flirting with young men.

"Thanks, but I can handle myself," Jackson replied with a chuckle. "When it comes to women, I'm not going to be with anyone I don't want to be with."

I held his gaze for a moment and then smiled. We removed our seat belts and settled in for what would most likely be a few hours of unproductive watching. After all, I strongly doubted Betty, Stella, Doris, or Madge would show up at Nona's Nugget. When several more young men came in, the older women, including Geraldine, practically pounced on them, then spoke and motioned their hands as if flirting and offering to buy drinks. Two of the men sat down at Geraldine's table, whereupon the waiter brought what appeared to be two beers, along with something for Geraldine—a tall, pink drink with flowers and fruit.

"I know I joke about the church single mingles, but I'm grateful we have safer ways to meet people," I said.

Jackson looked at me. "Yeah, those are better ways to meet people, although as someone older and single, I can tell you it's not always easy."

I winced inside. "I'm sorry. I shouldn't automatically assume it's easier for guys because they traditionally do the asking."

Jackson turned his gaze back to Geraldine, but it seemed he was seeing more than the desperate bar scene in front of us. "No problem, but thanks for saying that," he said. "I know a lot of effort goes into church single groups, but as I've gotten older I find it easier to meet people through trusted friends. If this weren't a bar and there was no alcohol, what we're watching could easily be a single mingle."

I chuckled but Jackson didn't.

"So, you haven't asked me the question," he said after a moment of silence.

"Question?"

"Why I'm thirty and still 'out there.'"

I twisted to see him better, with my feet propped up on the seat and my knees between us. "First of all, it's not that unusual for a thirty-year-old man to be single. Eventually I would like to hear about your past relationships, but when you tell me is your call."

He reached up and rubbed my knee. "I like you, Lizzy Langston."

I looked into his blue eyes and felt myself falling. "I like you, too," I said. "As much as I hate to admit it, I think Mr. Jonas did the right thing by asking you to help us."

"Well, it was my idea to have you work with me, so we can't give him all the credit."

I smiled and leaned my knees on the console. Jackson rested his arm comfortably on my knee.

"So tell me about all these attempts at finding Mr. Jonas a fine Christian woman. Our family has tried everything." Jackson smiled the dimple smile.

I told him about a few attempts at setting Mr. Jonas up and about my family's concerns that he hadn't been to church for years. Mr. Jonas always claimed he was too busy with work. Jackson shared a few of his family's efforts, and they, too, were worried that Mr. Jonas'd had a crisis of faith years ago with the loss of his wife. The Clark family wished they could do more, and I assured him that Mr. Jonas's absence from church hadn't gone unnoticed.

We kept an eye on Geraldine as she worked her way through drinks and younger men. Around 9:00 PM, she paid her bill and went to her car with one of the young guys. They stopped to kiss a few times as they walked to her Jaguar.

"So people really meet at bars and go home together?" I said more to myself than to Jackson.

"Yeah, they do."

I shook my head in disbelief. It seemed Geraldine might be spending the night with a man she barely knew. "I'm probably naive, but it's still shocking when you see stuff like this."

Jackson gave my hand a squeeze as we pulled out onto the street, following Geraldine. "I understand," he said.

"It's fair to say we were both raised with higher standards regarding personal relationships. Unfortunately, because of my job, I see a little more of the world than you do."

We followed Geraldine back to her house, and she and the young man went inside. Love pit or no love pit, he was going willingly.

As Jackson drove to Walmart, we made plans to watch Stella Perkins the next evening. She was an active Christian and the wife of a tractor repairman, so I imagined surveilling her would be radically different than what we had seen tonight.

Jackson pulled up alongside my car in the parking lot, and we talked for a while longer. He told me a few stories from his time on the police force. He'd seen some sad situations, most caused by poor choices, and he spoke about them candidly but with compassion.

When I said I had better go, he got out and helped me out of his car. We stood there for a moment, his gaze washing me in blue. He took my hands and wrapped them around his neck, then pulled me into his embrace. He smelled like sun-dried sheets and felt warm and familiar.

"Thank you, Lizzy," he whispered, and I knew what he meant. With my face buried in his neck, I could have stood there forever.

We pulled away at the same time, and he gently brushed the side of my face with his thumb. I held his hand against my face and closed my eyes, smiling.

"See you tomorrow," he said.

I opened my eyes and he reached for my car door.

"See you tomorrow."

Thirteen

Even though Stella Perkins lived on the opposite side of town, Jackson and I left my car at Walmart before we went to surveil her house. Preventing anyone from associating me with him and his car made the long drive worth it.

I wore capris, a green blouse, and sandals, with my hair piled on top of my head due to the heat. Jackson looked amazing in jeans and a light-purple button-down shirt. When I got into his car, the smell of his aftershave reminded me of our embrace—like I needed a reminder.

"Stella's husband, George, repairs tractors?" he said as he turned the car back toward Cutlip.

"Yep. No-nonsense people. Stalwart churchgoers. No miniskirts or Nona's Nugget for Stella."

Jackson nodded. "Hmm. From her email, it sounds like they had some sort of relationship with Oliver. Do you think maybe Mr. Perkins repaired Oliver's tractor?"

"Possibly. Stella mentioned how much Oliver loved his tractor, plus I don't know of anyone else around here who repairs tractors, other than a John Deere dealership in the city." I paused. "I always get the feeling the Perkinses aren't very happy. It seems like George stays busy repairing tractors to hide from Stella, and she makes sure everyone knows she resents it—that sort of thing."

"Interesting," Jackson said. We turned onto Main Street. Many businesses operated there, but what caught my eye was a group of older women dancing on the lawn of Gladys Ziggler's exercise studio. Their upbeat music was so loud it could be heard through the closed windows of Jackson's vehicle. I'd heard Gladys taught a Zumba class herself, so that had to be her facing the others, leading them in the moves. With a Stan's Air Conditioning truck out front, and a couple of men on the roof of the studio, it was obvious the air conditioning was broken, so Gladys had moved her class out to the lawn.

As my eyes focused on the women, it dawned on me. "Jackson, it's all of them—Gladys, Doris, Betty, Madge, Geraldine, and Stella!" I rolled down my window. My eyes locked with Gladys's just before the window started going up. I glanced sharply at Jackson, who still had his hand on the window controls from his side of the car. "Why did you do . . . Oh!" I put my hand over my mouth.

"Lizzy, do you know her?"

"No. I mean I know *of* her. I've seen her at church and around, and she probably knows who I am. But that's the connection—they're Zumba friends."

Jackson clearly didn't share my relief. "It looked like Mrs. Ziggler recognized you. In fact, she almost seemed to be expecting to see you."

"What do you mean?"

"It feels like we've been set up," Jackson said under his breath.

Panic rushed through me. "You mean she knows we've been watching her and the others? How? Plus there's no way she could know I'm the obituary writer."

"It's just a gut feeling." Jackson turned the corner and pulled into a parking lot, completely out of the Zumba ladies' sight. He grabbed his phone and started typing. A few seconds later, he said, "Okay, I've pulled up the website for Gladys's exercise studio and, let's see . . . list of classes." After a pause, he announced, "Yes, she teaches a 'Gray Is Great' Zumba class every Tuesday evening." Jackson looked at me and smiled. "I have an idea. Let me make this call over the Bluetooth so you can hear it."

After several rings, Mr. Jonas said hello. Jackson explained what had happened, and his hunch that Gladys was on to our investigation. Then he told my boss, "I need you to sign up for her Zumba class to see if anyone says anything about Oliver Moore."

There was a long, silent pause, during which I clamped my hand over my mouth to muffle my laughter at the thought of Mr. Jonas in a Zumba class.

"You want me to *what*?" my boss said finally, but it was more like a growl.

"I'll get some equipment and we'll wire you up so we can hear and see everything," Jackson said, ignoring the question. "You won't have to do anything."

"Won't have to do anything?" Mr. Jonas was almost shouting now. "I'll have to go dance around with a bunch of crazy ladies. I've heard about that Geraldine Nesbitt—I don't want to be anywhere near her."

I fought back my laughter, wondering just how much he knew about Geraldine.

Jackson cleared his throat. "I know it seems like a lot to ask, but I've learned to follow through on these hunches, and we really want to maintain Lizzy's anonymity." He paused, then added quietly, "We want to protect your delivery business, Abe, too."

Mr. Jonas huffed. "Well, if you think it's absolutely necessary, I'll sign up. But I'm only doing this once! Once—you hear me?"

"That should be enough to get the information we need," Jackson reassured him. He spent a few more minutes trying to calm Mr. Jonas, then ended the call.

"Oh goodness, that was funny," I said. Jackson and I both laughed, and then I asked, "So, should we do anything between now and next Tuesday?"

"All we have to do is wire Mr. Jonas for audio and sound." Jackson smiled. "We'll park around the corner from Gladys's studio, and we'll watch and listen to the action via my laptop. For now, I don't think we should surveil the women's houses. You should just go about your regular schedule like this encounter never happened. If you bump into Gladys or any of the other ladies, just act as you normally would." Jackson stopped and put his hand on my arm. "There is one thing you need to do, though."

I raised my eyebrows in question.

"Go to dinner with me Friday night?" he said.

"I'd love to."

He flashed a seriously cute smile, with dimples. Right then it dawned on me that with no more stakeouts, it would be a week until we'd see each other again. *Well, at least that will give me time to find something awesome to wear and get into JoEtta's for a trim—that's another obituary I need to share with Jackson sometime.*

"My parents own some property a couple of hours away, and I need to spend the next few days doing some work there," Jackson said, interrupting my musings. "But I'll be back on Friday, and we'll have a nice dinner." Jackson had mentioned his apartment in the city, but this was the first I'd heard of property in the country.

"So that's how you got these callouses," I said as I took his hand in both of mine and rubbed my thumbs across his palm. He chuckled.

"Yeah, my parents have a cabin on twenty acres, and I promised I'd keep an eye on it while they're gone."

Liking the fact that he knew which end of the shovel to use, I said, "Twenty acres is a fair chunk of land. It must be a lot of work."

"Yes, it is, especially when you're mending fences. It's beautiful, though. Maybe sometime I'll take you up and show you the property."

"I'd like that."

Jackson leaned closer and touched my cheek, but the sudden ringing of his phone broke the spell. He winked at me and answered the call via Bluetooth.

"What the heck do I wear to a Zumba class?" came the loud voice of my boss.

"Well, from what I saw, anything made of Spandex will do, and sequins couldn't hurt," Jackson replied without missing a beat.

JoEtta Coons
1938–2013

JoEtta Coons died in her sleep at the age of seventy-five. She married poorly out of high school, but quickly divorced and took back her maiden name. She named her daughter LaDell and said the girl was the "only thing good to come from it all." JoEtta's family lived in Tennessee, so the women of Cutlip pitched in and helped watch LaDell while JoEtta put herself through beauty school. She paid them all back by opening and running—for over fifty years—the best place in Cutlip to "get yourself done up," JoEtta's Beauty Salon.

JoEtta was popular among the older women for her "tight little perms," and word of her skills traveled far and wide. This fame allowed her to provide a comfortable living for herself and LaDell, who followed in her mother's cosmetology footsteps. It is at the request of LaDell that I compose this obituary, to explain the details of her mother's death, and to thank the kind women of Cutlip.

As JoEtta "came along in years" she took to napping while her clients' perms processed. Rolling the tiny rods "just so" took time and energy, and the attention to detail began to tire JoEtta out. Therefore, she would apply the perm chemicals to "do their magic," make sure her client was settled with a magazine and a Coke, then slip in the back room for a little nap. But a week ago Thursday, as JoEtta gave Sarah Sewell a perm, LaDell noticed her mother looked a little "peaked." LaDell helped her finish *rolling the rods and apply the chemicals, then sent her mom off to her nap in the back room . . . which is where LaDell found her two hours later. LaDell had been busy with her own clients and hadn't noticed her mother's absence until Sarah came to her, "scalp ablaze" from overprocessing. They discovered JoEtta in her recliner, having passed away in her sleep.*

LaDell, who will continue running JoEtta's Beauty Salon, wishes to thank the women of Cutlip for their "kind and loyal patronage." LaDell says her mother "died with a smile on her face," knowing Sarah Sewell's perm was going to be practically perfect. Unfortunately, this was not the case, for Sarah's hair was fried off right down to the roots. LaDell would like to thank Etta's Wigs, which has kindly offered to provide Sarah with free wigs until her hair grows back. Sarah isn't worried, though, claiming that even though she's bald, "it was an honor to be JoEtta's last perm."

Fourteen

Tuesday and Wednesday each felt like a week long. I had told Hannah what I could—that I had a dinner date with Jackson on Friday, that I was getting a haircut and a new dress for it, and that I was really starting to like this guy. To celebrate, she took me shopping and to lunch. We found a pretty pale-blue dress, and the best part was I already had shoes and jewelry that would look great with it. I spent a relaxing hour at JoEtta's, where LaDell trimmed my hair and did a hot oil treatment to make it shine.

Jackson said he would drive his truck on our date so I wouldn't need to worry about being spotted in his work car. I hadn't realized he had a truck, but it made sense considering he helped out at his parents' country property.

When Friday finally arrived, I was super nervous, which seemed ridiculous, since I had spent hours with Jackson, surveilling old ladies all over Cutlip and beyond. But this was our first official date. I kept redoing my hair and eventually decided to pile it high on my head in loose curls so I wouldn't play with it throughout the evening. When the doorbell rang, I had to stop myself from running. I opened the door and there he stood, looking very handsome in dress pants and a gray-blue button-down shirt. He held a gorgeous bouquet of daisies, which he handed to me, saying, "You look beautiful, Lizzy."

"Wow, these are so pretty. I love daisies."

Jackson smiled and walked into the house. "I guess I'm a little old-fashioned about some things."

"Well, I'm glad." I led him into the kitchen. "Come and help me put them in some water."

"This is a great house," he said.

"Yeah. It's quite old—one of the first homes built in the area. My parents bought it not long after they got married, and it was really rundown. I can't remember a time when some remodeling project wasn't going on."

I got a white porcelain vase down from a shelf and filled it with water. The daisies were from Honeychurch Flowers—which reminded me of another obituary I wanted to share with Jackson. I thanked him for bringing the daisies, which looked stunning in the vase. I felt his gaze on me as I set the vase on the dining table. When I turned to him, he reached for my hand and pulled me close. As I moved into his arms, my mind shut off. All I did was feel—his hands on my back, my fingers on his stiff collar, my cheek brushing against his smoothly shaven skin. And best of all, his warm, soft lips on mine. It all happened in one motion and I couldn't stop it—not that I wanted to. The air and light around us felt different, a new space that was just ours.

I don't know how long we kissed, since time seemed to have stopped. Our lips came apart but just barely as we inhaled the same air. I pulled away to look at him and said with a smile, "So, you're not completely old-fashioned."

Jackson kissed me again. "No, not completely," he whispered against my lips and we both chuckled. He stepped back slightly and swept his gaze over my face, stopping at my mouth. He outlined my lips with his thumb, the roughness of his skin making me tingle. "I just couldn't wait any longer." He gave me a quick kiss and drew me into an embrace. I closed my eyes, melting into him.

As he held me his lips moved to my ear. "So I take it you're not dating anyone else."

I managed to mumble, "Uh . . . no."

"Good. Do you mind keeping it that way?"

"Yes, as long as you don't date anyone else either."

We both laughed a little at my response.

"You as hungry as I am?" Jackson asked.

"Starving."

"Good. I was going to take you to Morton's for steak—does that sound okay?" He paused. "I mean, you eat meat, right?"

"Oh, it sounds like you've dated a few vegetarians."

"Let's just say there was a very awkward date with a Yoga instructor."

"I love steak, and Morton's sounds great," I told him.

We walked out onto the front porch and headed to his gray Chevy Silverado. With a tool box and trailer hitch, it was obviously used for real work, but it was clean and shiny. Jackson helped me into the truck, which was pretty tidy on the inside, too.

After he pulled out onto the street, he rested his right hand on the console, so I took his fingers in my left hand.

Being with him felt safe and comfortable, yet my stomach turned with excitement at the memory of his lips on mine. I studied his profile as he drove and told me about his work on his parents' property.

Morton's was beautiful, with candlelight and quiet, cozy booths. We ate Porterhouse steaks with salad and creamy potatoes, then shared a piece of chocolate lava cake. Jackson talked about his trip to New Zealand with his parents, then explained how challenging it was to change his degree from international finance to criminal justice, but how much he enjoyed solving crimes. I told him about my decision to teach math and how much I loved for things to add up. He laughed at that, but said he understood. We lost track of time and were some of the last customers to leave the restaurant.

Back at my house, we sat on the front porch swing. The moonlight made everything appear shiny, or maybe it was my imagination. Jackson wrapped his arm around my shoulder and pulled me in. It seemed as if we'd sat this way many times before, though of course we hadn't. The thought of him kissing me again sent shivers through me.

We sat in comfortable silence for a while, watching the breeze sway the draping branches of the two weeping willows, one tree guarding each corner of the front lawn.

"Your grass needs mowing. Do you have someone do that?" Jackson asked out of the blue. I could feel his breath against my hair.

"Yes, the name is Lizzy's Lawn Service, and they're scheduled to mow it tomorrow morning." I let out a deep breath. On one of our stakeouts, I'd mentioned my attempts to make money before I landed the newspaper-carrier job with Mr. Jonas. I had definitely spent too much time behind a mower.

"Can I come and help you mow it tomorrow?" Jackson said.

I stopped the swing and turned to look at him. "You'd do that?"

He smiled. "Of course, but you'll have to feed me after."

"You got yourself a deal." I took his face in my hands and drew his lips to mine. He pulled me closer and kissed me for a few minutes. When it was time for him to leave, he unlocked my front door and opened it for me, then kissed me once more. He waited for me to lock up and turn some lights on before he pulled out of the drive. Even though it was late, I called my parents to tell them about Jackson.

John Honeychurch
1949–2011

John Honeychurch died at the age of sixty-two from a heart attack. He and his beloved wife, Analu, had been married for forty-three years, the same length of time they had owned and operated Honeychurch Flowers, a popular business.

John and Analu worked well together. Analu, a creative genius at arranging flowers, always had her clippers and vases at the ready. With a mind for business, John took all the floral orders and handled the books. Flower shipments came in regularly, and orders were filled and delivered promptly. Honeychurch Flowers was an example of small-business efficiency. One need only call and tell John what you wanted to send. Of course he would ask, "What would you like to say on the card?" That's where things went terribly off-track. The family has requested my services in an attempt to make amends.

Upon John's untimely death, their daughter, Nellie, stepped in to take over her father's responsibilities. A short perusal of the order history produced a clear and shocking history of the "editing" John did on some of the floral cards. He would write the sentiment the customer wanted on one side, then add his own thoughts on the other side. He kept an accurate record of all of these, tracking trends and calculating successes.

For example, birthdays are a popular time to send flowers, but one sentiment that read "Happy Birthday to our beloved mother" had John's added comment "In my experience, the use of 'beloved' in a flower order implies a strained parent-child relationship. Also, your son phoned in this order while at the race track—he was very preoccupied. When asked what type of flowers he wanted to send, he growled, "Just throw something together.'"

Flowers are a must for wedding anniversaries. One card read: "Happy Anniversary to my wife of many years—may there be many more to come." Apparently John took this order in person, because his added sentiment read: "When I asked this joker what flowers would match your personality, he started looking through the shop for a cactus. I charged him extra for the roses, just so you know."

Of course Valentine's Day was a busy time at Honeychurch Flowers, yet John still found time to add his own thoughts to several cards. When one man ordered flowers for his wife and was asked how he wanted the card to read, he said, "To the love of my life, Happy Valentine's Day," to which John added: "It took this jerk ten full minutes to figure out what to write. He finally copied this off a helium balloon we had in the shop. He did, by the way, place another flower order in which he mentioned something about you being gone to your mother's next weekend. I'd check that out if I were you."

Words cannot describe the deep humiliation and regret the Honeychurch family feels. They offer their most sincere apologies to all of Cutlip. Nellie, trusted member of the PTA and longtime notary public, will oversee all written sentiment from now on.

Fifteen

As I opened the shed door to grab the lawn mower and weed eater, I heard Jackson's truck pull up on the street out front. Under the overcast sky, the humid air smelled spicy, thanks to the fig tree in our back yard. I had on my work clothes—cutoffs, an old T-shirt, and tennis shoes. My messy hair was thrown into a ponytail.

Jackson walked around the corner of the house, wearing jeans, T-shirt, baseball cap, and the determined gaze of a man ready to work. I could almost see him making a mental check list of things to do, something I'd experienced a hundred times with my dad and brothers.

When Jackson spotted me, he smiled and hurried over. "Morning, gorgeous," he said as he took the gas can out of my hands. I winced at his compliment, knowing I looked dramatically different than the evening before. He must not have cared, because he took my arms and wrapped them around his neck, then drew me close and said softly in my ear, "How's my Lizzy Girl this morning?"

Parts of me melted at the simple words. I kissed him soundly, then pulled away. "I'm good. It's so sweet of you to help me."

He flashed his dimples. "How about you start on the weed eater and I'll get the mower going?"

He checked the weed eater for line and fuel, then started it and handed it to me. I moved to the edge of the lawn. Jackson started the mower with one pull and began a systematic pattern across the grass. I liked doing the lawn work by myself, but this was even better, moving in a comfortable rhythm alongside a person who knew how to work.

Before I knew it we were done, and the lawn looked great. I'd set my alarm extra early to cut up fresh fruit and make pancake batter, and when Jackson started spraying off the walks, I told him I'd go make breakfast. When he came into the kitchen, his hands and face were dripping with water, so I handed him a towel before I flipped the last few pancakes.

"Thanks. I washed off with the hose," Jackson said. "This smells great, Lizzy. You've gone to some extra trouble." He leaned against the stove and dried his neck with the towel. He looked so good I almost dropped the spatula.

"You didn't have to help with the yard," I managed.

He reached over and pulled a leaf from my hair. "It was fun."

I handed him the plate of pancakes, then went to the fridge for the fruit. "These are special pancakes, from Ida Sue's cookbook. Did I ever tell you about that obituary?"

"No. Is it funny?" Jackson asked.

"Yeah, although the way she died sounds pretty awful." The daisies were still perky, so I had put them on the table in their vase. Jackson set the pancakes down and waited by my side of the table. I smiled and allowed him to pull out the chair for me.

After I said a blessing on the food, we ate our breakfast. Then I pulled out my phone and read him the obituary.

Ida Sue Faircloth
1924–2008

Ida Sue Faircloth died tragically at the age of eight-four. She was bludgeoned to death by the lid of her pressure canner, which malfunctioned and exploded during a processing cycle. Her sister Lucretia found Ida Sue on the floor of her kitchen, face-down on a mound of dilly beans.

Ida Sue was praised far and wide for her original recipes and her cooking prowess. She received blue ribbons from county and state fairs for everything from pickled pearl onions to her triple-death chocolate cream pie. Her reputation as Cutlip's finest cook was unchallenged—until now. Lucretia found some interesting things in Ida Sue's kitchen and has requested my services to share them.

A few years ago, after much begging and pleading from several prestigious women's organizations, Ida Sue finally agreed to share her culinary secrets with the masses by penning a cookbook. It sold like hot cakes, and she made a small fortune. Women who got their hands on it raced home, eager to be the first to make Ida Sue's cherry chutney or her cream-cheese croissants. Phone lines in Cutlip were burning up, everyone wanting to know who was making what. As cooks donned their aprons and entered their kitchens, a hush fell over the town.

The hush lasted way too long, finally turning into a bloated, tense silence. No woman emerged from her kitchen standing victorious over her chicken fricassee, or proud and ready to serve her family a perfectly fluffy lemon soufflé. No, it was a quiet week in Cutlip, other than the gritting of teeth and the scraping of food into the garbage can, and maybe the occasional frustrated scream.

The dawn of the next day found many cooks returning to grocery stores, buying more ingredients and wearing determined looks as they loaded the groceries into their cars. As the story goes, they went home to try a second and third and fourth time, only to fail and end up slinging the mistakes to the dogs.

Ida Sue's phone began to ring, as she knew it would, with desperate cooks wanting to know why the dishes they had made from her book hadn't turned out; after all, they had followed the recipes exactly. Ida Sue would sweetly say something akin to "Well, my dear, it must be my special touch." However, once the funeral was over, Lucretia discovered that Ida Sue had purposely omitted one key ingredient from each recipe in her cookbook. Thus, the recipes, every last one of them, were doomed to failure. Apparently, Ida Sue wanted to remain the queen of Cutlip cooking.

Lucretia has, of course, agreed to reprint her sister's cookbook with the complete recipes. People *who purchased the original cookbook and have the emotional wherewithal to try one more time are welcome to contact Lucretia for a free copy of the corrected version.*

"So she really left stuff out of all her recipes?" Jackson asked.

"Yep. It was quite the scandal," I said. "Lucretia was really sweet about it and tried to make sure everyone got a corrected cookbook."

"Well, I have to admit, as devious as Ida Sue was, she makes a mean pancake," he said, starting in on his fifth.

We ate and talked and laughed. Time seemed to fly, and suddenly it was after 12:00. My homework was calling me, and Jackson needed to run some errands, so he helped clean up the kitchen and then took off, but not before we made plans to go to a movie that evening.

The rest of the weekend went by like a dream. After church I cooked dinner for him, and we spent Sunday evening talking on the front porch. I didn't know where our relationship was going, but I was definitely falling for Jackson.

We used Jackson's work car on Tuesday evening, since it was equipped for surveillance. We all met up in the Walmart parking lot. Jackson and I arrived first. He opened his car door, and I slid into the front seat. As soon as he got in the driver's side, he leaned over and kissed me. The taste of his lips sent a wave of happiness through me. We pulled apart but rested our foreheads together.

"Missed you," he whispered, then kissed me again. The passionate kiss almost made me forget where I was. We both jumped when a tap sounded on Jackson's window. He rolled it down.

"Sorry to interrupt, but Zumba class starts pretty soon," Mr. Jonas said with equal parts curiosity and sarcasm. He was wearing a pair of basketball shorts and a T-shirt. "I believe you need to wire me up or something."

Jackson unlocked the back doors, and he and Mr. Jonas got into the back seat. "I have all the stuff here," Jackson said. He removed some wires and tape from a bag. "We'll tape these to your chest. This small pin is the camera. Lizzy and I will be able to see and hear everything you see and hear, but since we want you to act as normal as possible, we won't have you wear an earpiece. That means you won't be able to hear Lizzy and me. The whole idea is for the ladies to be comfortable enough to talk to you."

I tried to muffle a laugh. "I heard that, Lizzy," Mr. Jonas said.

"Now if you'll take your shirt off, I'll tape these wires to your chest and put the pin on your shirt." Jackson sounded so professional.

"I can't believe I'm doing this," Mr. Jonas muttered.

To give him some privacy I faced forward again, but never having seen a person get wired, I couldn't resist a peek in the rearview mirror. I should have resisted, though. Who knew Mr. Jonas was so hairy?

"Okay, try to build rapport with these women," Jackson said. "Get them to take you under their wing, to trust you. Then maybe they'll give us a clue about what happened to Mr. Moore. We'll park a block away and watch and listen via the computer. Whatever you do, don't let the women find these wires, because then you'll look like a . . ."

"Pervert," Mr. Jonas finished. I bit back a giggle. He readjusted his wires as if trying to get comfortable. "Okay, okay," he said. "I'm going and I'll meet you back here after the class." As he climbed out of the car, he mumbled, "What I won't do to save my newspaper."

Jackson got back in the driver's seat, and we followed Mr. Jonas's old truck back toward town.

We pulled into an office parking lot one street over, and Jackson set up his laptop and connected remotely to the receptors on Mr. Jonas's chest. The picture came into focus as he walked into the exercise studio. Seconds later, Gladys Ziggler's face filled the screen. She wore a microphone headset.

"Well, hello, Abe."

"Hi, Gladys. I signed up for the Zumba class," Mr. Jonas said, sounding defeated.

"Wonderful!" remarked Geraldine Nesbitt, her face popping onto the screen. "It's the Gray Is Great class, and you'll certainly fit right in with your wonderfully full head of gray hair." She wore black leggings, a tank top, and a sequined chiffon skirt. "Come with me and I'll introduce you to everyone."

Mr. Jonas uttered something under his breath as he followed her into the Zumba room. Jackson and I gasped when we saw the wall-to-wall mirrors. Fortunately Mr. Jonas couldn't hear us.

Betty, Stella, Doris, and Madge were there as well. By the looks on their faces as Geraldine introduced Mr. Jonas, no man had ever entered their inner sanctum.

"Ladies, we are honored to have Abraham Jonas, owner of the *Cutlip Currier,* with us tonight," Gladys announced.

"Let's make him feel welcome and give him a little help." With that, she blasted some salsa music. Immediately, she and the other women swayed their hips like it was the most natural thing in the world. Mr. Jonas slowly began to move his hips in a poor attempt at rhythm.

"A little more action in those hips, Abe," Gladys said. At the sound of her voice booming through the speakers with the music, Mr. Jonas jumped. He tried to do as he was told, but it looked like he had a bug in his shorts.

Suddenly, Geraldine's face appeared on the computer screen in front of Jackson and Lizzy. "Here, let me show you how you should move your hips. It needs to be a more fluid motion." Geraldine reached for Mr. Jonas.

He jumped away. "More fluid. Okay, I got it." He motioned for her to move back.

"Don't be afraid, Abe. You need to get in touch with your body." Geraldine tried to grab his hips.

"Back off, Geraldine," Gladys said over the music.

Geraldine smiled and winked at Mr. Jonas, then moved in front of him and began swinging and swaying in an exaggerated example of how it should be done. The other women frowned in disgust.

When the music changed to a techno swing, the steps got more complicated. Now Mr. Jonas breathed heavily. Sweat poured off his arms, and large portions of his T-shirt looked soaked. Obviously, he was struggling to keep up.

"Abe, darling, just keep your eyes on my hips and you'll do just fine." Geraldine sounded like a huntress luring her prey.

Suddenly, there was a loud grunt, and then the grains of a hardwood floor filled the screen just before it went too dark to see anything. The music stopped, two women screamed, and Geraldine said under her breath, "Not again."

Movement and voices mixed in a chaotic scramble as Mr. Jonas got back on his feet. "I'm fine ladies, just fine," he assured them. "Maybe I'm going to have to ease into this Zumba stuff." He started making his way to the door.

"Let me get you some water," Gladys offered nervously.

"I have some in my truck," Mr. Jonas replied. "I'll be fine, I promise. I'm calling it an evening, though. You ladies have fun." He made his way out the door.

Half a minute later, Mr. Jonas climbed into his truck and said quietly, "I think we got what we need." The last sound we heard before our screen went blank was his scream.

Ooh, I guess it hurt to rip the wires off his hairy chest, I thought, then said to Jackson, "So maybe Mr. Moore had his heart attack at Zumba?"

Jackson scratched his forehead. "Could be. It would explain the clothing change. But why not just call 9-1-1? Why hide the fact that he died at Zumba? I'm afraid I'm going to have to talk to them."

Just then, Jackson's phone rang. It was Mr. Jonas, confirming that we'd heard what Geraldine said.

"I'm going to have to find out if Mr. Moore died at the studio," Jackson told my boss. "And if so, we need to know why they moved his body and staged the death elsewhere. After all, they could end up in jail for breaking the law." Jackson paused, then blew out a breath. "Let me think about it for a day and see if I can come up with something that won't risk Lizzy's anonymity."

"Well, I'm not going back to that class," I heard Mr. Jonas say through the phone.

Jackson and I smiled. "I don't know," he said. "Geraldine was pretty attractive. And she can obviously dance."

There was a long pause before Mr. Jonas barked, "I'll bring the equipment by tomorrow," and hung up.

Jackson put his phone in his pocket. "If I could interview Gladys, maybe make a deal with her, we can find out the truth and still keep your secret."

I smiled, but I couldn't shake the feeling this wasn't going to turn out well. A few of Jackson's kisses and a hug in the Walmart parking lot took my mind off things. As I drove home, Geraldine's words kept playing through my brain. "Not again," she'd said.

Minutes later, I pulled into the driveway. I got out of my car and headed for the front porch, but a piece of paper on the side kitchen door caught my eye. I rushed over, took down the note, and read:

Miss Langston,

I know who you are, obituary writer. Stop poking around my Zumba class or I will expose you.

Just so you know, many people who have provoked my family haven't lived to tell about it.

Gladys Ziggler

I got back in my car, locked the doors, and called Jackson.

Sixteen

"How did she find out I'm the obituary writer?" I buried my head in Jackson's chest. Tears burned in my eyes. He had made it back in impressive time and insisted on checking the entire house before I went inside. His sweep of every room didn't seem necessary, since I doubted Gladys had done anything but leave the note. Of course, that was enough to shake me, with the veiled death threat and all.

"I don't know, but we'll find out and it will be okay, I promise," Jackson replied, stroking my hair. I heard a tap and then the front door opened.

"Lizzy, are you all right?"

I moved into Mr. Jonas's arms almost before he could ask the question. He hugged me and then pulled away to look at me.

"Just shaken up a bit," I said. "I'm so sorry. I don't know how this happened."

"Oh, it's all right. You didn't do anything wrong. We'll figure this out and everything will be fine." Despite the way he often teased me, I knew he felt protective of me like a daughter.

He handed me some tissues that Jackson had retrieved from the kitchen. "Come and sit down here and we'll talk," Mr. Jonas said, and I followed him to the sofa. Jackson handed me a glass of water and sat in a chair across from us. I drank it all and felt a bit better.

Jackson snapped into detective mode. "Lizzy, let's go back through a few situations where Gladys could have realized you write the obituaries. I don't know that it will do us any good, but it will give you some peace of mind."

The three of us talked for a while about all the possible ways Gladys could have learned my identity, but none seemed likely. When we found ourselves back to where we started, Mr. Jonas said to me, "Why don't I spend some time tomorrow and see what I can find out about Gladys, and I bet Jackson will do the same."

"Of course, definitely," I said.

"I'll check out her background on the databases I can access at the station," Jackson said. After a pause, he added, "At some point this needs to be turned into an official case, but I would like to have some evidence first or it will go nowhere. Since I know both of you, the case wouldn't be assigned to me. Plus, as you know, I didn't immediately report the emails you received about the circumstances of Oliver's death. That delay might cost me an official reprimand. But we don't know if Oliver's body was actually moved, so therefore we have no proof these women broke the law. If his body wasn't disturbed, someone is playing a really clever joke on you, Lizzy, or even on you, Abe. The women could also be charged with tampering with evidence. When someone isn't known to have been ill and wasn't under the care of a doctor, and when there is no obvious cause of death, the immediate area is usually treated as a crime scene. It's pretty routine. If the women messed with Mr. Moore's body or other evidence, they have broken the law. Long story short, the timing of involving the police department could be tricky, so let me worry about that."

We agreed to meet back at my house the next evening. Mr. Jonas insisted on staying for a while, to make sure I felt safe. He said he would "rest" for a while on the sofa until around 4:00 AM, when he would need to return to the newspaper office.

As Jackson moved toward the front door, I said, "Wait, I'll walk you out."

He grinned and took my hand.

Mr. Jonas cleared his throat. "Mr. Clark, that's a very special young woman you have there. Are your intentions honorable?"

"They are, sir," Jackson answered with a chuckle before he and I stepped out onto the porch.

When we reached his truck I sank into his embrace. After a minute, he pulled back and kissed me softly. "This will work out, Lizzy."

I agreed but without conviction. "Your hunch was right—about Gladys recognizing me when we drove by."

"Yes, she must have. But don't worry." He took me in his arms again. I kissed him and said good night.

I walked back into the house and sat across from Mr. Jonas, who was writing something on his ever-present notepad.

"You like him, don't you?" he asked.

"Yeah, I like him a lot," I answered.

Mr. Jonas gave me a victorious smile. I couldn't help but smile back. He looked thoughtful for a moment, then said, "Jackson is a good man and I trust him completely. Has he told you about his past?"

I shook my head. "He brought it up when we talked about him being thirty and unmarried, but I told him I'd wait until he felt ready to tell me."

"That's wise. I promise it's nothing to worry about. Just keep in mind that he has been through a great deal and is wiser than his years."

I nodded and yawned at the same time.

"Now go get some sleep, Lizzy. We'll see what we can snoop out and make a plan tomorrow evening. Then you should call your parents and tell them what's going on. Now go."

"Okay, I'm going," I grumbled and went upstairs. Almost as soon as I closed my eyes, I fell asleep.

Seventeen

"It's like she didn't exist before she came to America," Mr. Jonas said, thumbing through a pile of papers. He had spent hours searching for relevant information on Gladys. He arrived at my house early, so while we waited for Jackson, my boss and I went over what he had found. "All I know is she came to America in 1944 at age fifteen," Mr. Jonas reported. "And not long after that she married Jacob Ziggler, who also emigrated in 1944. How they got out of Germany during the war would be a great story on its own. The name on her marriage license was Gladys Braun. I couldn't even find out what part of Germany she came from."

He buried his head in his papers again. Thanks to the internet, it was almost impossible to hide this type of information, but somehow Gladys had managed to do so.

My thoughts were interrupted by a knock at the door. I hollered for Jackson to come in.

"Sorry I'm a little late, but I have good news," he said, looking harried and handsome. He had a rather thick file in his hand. He sat down and handed us each a packet of papers.

"Using one of the databases at work, I found some info and printed it out for us. She was born Gladys Braun in 1929 in Dingelstädt, Germany." A small grin crept across Jackson's face.

"That's a strange name," Mr. Jonas said.

"It's for real," Jackson confirmed. "She came to America with Jacob Ziggler. I have copies of documents showing them being processed through customs at the same time. They were married not too long after arriving in America. I had to really dig for some of this information and still couldn't find anything about Gladys or her family in Germany—no parents or siblings or anything."

"Do you think records were lost or destroyed in the war?" I asked.

"That's a possibility, but usually when you're dealing with a whole family, records show up somewhere online. Somebody went to a great deal of effort to make sure there is no evidence of Gladys Braun or her family in Germany."

"How can that be, in this age of technology?" I said.

"It's hard to imagine, but in small towns there's still a good amount of information that never makes it to the internet—just ask a genealogist. Add in the fact that someone obviously didn't want this information out there, and you have the situation we're in," Mr. Jonas replied.

Jackson nodded in confirmation. "I explained the whole situation to Sergeant Perdue in detail. Even though this isn't an official case, he'll allow me to use department resources. Plus, he's letting me take off some personal time if I need to. He also said to tell you hello, Mr. Jonas."

"He's a good friend of mine," was all my boss said. I made a mental note to ask Jackson if he knew just how close our bosses were.

"Sergeant Perdue said that since there seem to be no electronic trails left by the Braun family, it will require some old-school, boots-on-the-ground sort of detective work," Jackson said. This brought a grin to Mr. Jonas's face.

"So what does this mean?" I asked, remembering Sergeant Perdue's reputation for unusual investigation methods.

"I have a good friend from Germany. I met him in college when I studied international finance. We remained close—even did some humanitarian missions together." After glancing at Mr. Jonas with an expression I didn't understand, Jackson added, "His name is Markus Bauer, and he's willing to help us."

"Does he have a way of finding these records?" I asked.

"Well, yes, but not how you would think. Because he grew up in Germany, he understands small communities like Dingelstädt and believes the only way to find out about the Braun family would be to do it in person, to actually talk to people. This is the type of traditional detective work Sergeant Perdue was talking about. There are paper records somewhere but it might take us weeks to find them. In a few days of asking around, we could probably find out what Gladys is hiding. Markus is in Germany now visiting family, but he's willing to take a few days to go to Dingelstädt with me. I speak a little German, but he's fluent of course, so many people would trust him.

"The sergeant will keep an eye on Gladys just in case she decides to take off. He's given us some time and resources to figure this out, but that doesn't mean he isn't taking her threat and conduct seriously. There will be consequences for all this. He wants to know what happened to Oliver Moore, or if the emails are part of an elaborate hoax. The sergeant also mentioned that he hopes the secret obituary writer is still in business when his mother-in-law passes. He's taken care of her for several years, apparently not an easy task, and he's hoping to get a few things off his chest with one of your obituaries.

I grinned at that, but then asked in a serious tone, "So you're willing to go all the way to Germany to help us? Why are you being so generous, Jackson?"

"We really do need to find out what happened the day Mr. Moore died. Plus we need to make sure the obituaries continue, to keep the newspaper going. But it's not just about saving Abe's business. Lizzy, what you do for this community is special. Sure, as a detective I like to get the bad guys, but it is also important to help the good guys who make a difference." Jackson's eyes met mine, and my heart took one big step closer to his.

Mr. Jonas practically beamed. "Lizzy, why don't you go with him? I've been saving points on the business credit card forever. If I convert them to sky miles, there's probably enough to fly both of you over there."

"What? Go to Germany? I can't just drop everything and go to Germany."

"Why not? You probably have A's in all your classes, and you haven't used any of your vacation time. Take a few days and go with Jackson."

"I don't know," I said. "I have finals, too." I had never been afraid to take a risk, but it was one thing to be the only girl newspaper carrier in town, and another thing entirely to fly to Germany on a whim.

"Lizzy, why don't you call your parents and talk this over with them?" Jackson said. "I'll be happy to speak with them as well. I wouldn't want my daughter flying halfway around the world with someone I didn't know. And if you don't feel comfortable with this, I completely understand. But I would really like it if you came with me. I would love you to meet Markus—he's like a brother to me."

I smiled at Jackson and let his blue eyes calm me.

"I'll talk to your parents, too, Lizzy, and they'll be all right with this, I think," said Mr. Jonas. "You're due an adventure and old enough to decide to have one, and it couldn't be with a more trusted and capable young man. And the fact is, I need you to go be the journalist I'm paying you to be. You've learned to understand people. Take that knowledge and help me save my company."

"Okay. Let's call my parents," I said.

Eighteen

Sitting between Jackson and Mr. Jonas, I made the call, with my cell phone on speaker. We introduced Jackson to my mom and dad, then explained that Gladys Ziggler had somehow discovered I was the obituary writer. As the conversation progressed, my parents seemed to like Jackson. My boss's triumphant glances confirmed this feeling.

Finally, I took a deep breath and explained that Jackson planned to travel to Germany to search for information that would help us figure out what happened to Oliver Moore. I asked my parents what they thought of my going on the trip, where, of course, Jackson and I would have separate hotel rooms.

After a pause, my father said he trusted me to make my own decision, and my mom agreed. Their confidence in my choices sent a thrill of gratitude through me. Whether or not I went on the trip, my parents knew I'd stick to my moral standards. I thanked Mom and Dad and promised to send them a copy of our itinerary.

We ended the conference call with my dad wishing us success, and my mom warning Jackson that if anything happened to me, she'd hunt him down and kill him with her bare hands. Mr. Jonas and I laughed. Jackson did too, but with a bit of uncertainty.

"I'll get online and look at flights," Jackson said after the call.

"I've accumulated a ton of points on my business credit card, so I bet you both can fly business class and rent a car."

"I hate to use your points," I replied. "I'm sure you were planning an exotic trip of some kind." Knowing Mr. Jonas rarely went on vacation, I gave him a teasing smile.

He shook his head. "Use the points, Lizzy. And remember, I'm expecting you to come home with something on Gladys." Mr. Jonas turned to Jackson. "Give me a call when you see what's available and we'll work it out." Then my boss excused himself and went back to work.

Jackson and I sat on the sofa again. He wrapped his arm around me and pulled me closer, then said, "Your parents seem very nice."

I rested my head on his shoulder. "They like you—I can tell." I paused. "You know, for all my talk about being independent, the truth is, I've really missed my parents. This is the closest I've come to living on my own."

"They obviously trust you and love you," Jackson said. At my smile, he added, "That thing your mom mentioned, about killing me with her bare hands. Was it for real?"

I chuckled. "Absolutely."

—∞∞∞—

Our flight was early in the morning, and the airport smelled like a swirl of foods. My stomach grumbled in response. I'd been too nervous and excited to eat much, so I was counting on all the fabulous food Mr. Jonas promised would be served in business class. I had flown a few times, mainly short flights to neighboring states, so spending over twelve hours on an airplane would be a new experience.

My professors had allowed me to take my finals early, so the excitement of this trip was coupled with the relief of finishing the semester. Getting time off from the tutoring lab required some juggling, but I worked it out.

As for my best friend, I told Hannah I would be gone for a few days. Of course she assumed I was going to Toronto to visit my parents, and I didn't correct her. I wanted to tell her I was heading to Germany with Jackson, but that would bring up questions I couldn't answer without breaking other promises.

"You look worried. Is everything okay?" asked Jackson. We had gone through security, found a couple of seats, and were waiting to board the plane. He had obviously just shaved and looked amazing in jeans and a navy-blue pullover. I wore leggings and a long, comfy tunic, since we'd be on the plane for so many hours.

"Just thinking about Hannah," I replied. "It bothers me to not be honest with her. It's always bugged me that I couldn't tell her I'm the secret obituary writer, but this feels like a big lie."

Jackson nodded. "It is a big one and will take some maneuvering. If it's any help, I understand. I've worked a couple of undercover jobs—nothing big, but enough to really bother me about keeping it from those in my life."

"You worked undercover?" I asked softly, as if my normal volume would threaten his cover. "As what?"

Jackson chuckled. "I can't tell you details or names, but they were white-collar crimes dealing with corporations and embezzlement. I posed as an executive to catch businessmen who were stealing their company's money."

"So, no bushy beards and long hair posing as a South American drug lord?" I smirked.

"Nope. I did grow a mustache for one job, though. Does that count?"

"A little." I laughed. *He'd look good with a mustache.*

The airline called for boarding of our flight to New York. A minute later, Jackson and I settled into our comfortable, roomy seats in first class. Right away a flight attendant asked for our drink orders; she seemed a bit surprised when we both ordered orange juice. Once the plane reached cruising altitude, she served us a delicious breakfast. Jackson and I took our time eating while he told me more stories about his undercover work.

After the flight attendant whisked away our food trays, the woman across the aisle removed a book from her carry-on and began to read. The cover caught my eye, and I stifled a gasp. Fabio's bare chest took up almost half of the cover as he embraced a buxom damsel who clearly had been overcome.

"Want to hear about another obituary I wrote?" I asked Jackson. He answered with a mischievous smile and a raised eyebrow. "See the book that woman is reading?" I whispered, then subtly drew his attention across the aisle.

Jackson glanced at the cover and then back at me. That's when I told him about Cutlip's most shocking obituary—one that rocked the town and was still a topic of conversation among some residents.

"So your dead mayor wrote that book . . . with Fabio on the cover?" Jackson asked.

"He did, and eighty-seven others. Although I never read any," I assured with a knowing look. "They were quite popular, though. Our librarian, Ms. Clonts, started the Bobo Book Club, which meets at the library once a month to discuss his novels. I hear the discussions can get quite steamy." I whispered the last part.

Jackson laughed so loudly that a couple of passengers turned to stare at us. "I bet if Sophronia Cutlip had been alive when this came out," he managed to say, "she would have cut him off from her holiday fruit cakes."

"Yep. So fast his head would spin. She's probably still flipping over in her grave."

The flight attendant asked Jackson and me if we'd like some coffee. We declined, ordering a Diet Pepsi for me, and a regular one for him. But the mention of coffee reminded me of another rather shocking obituary.

"You know how Mormons aren't supposed to drink coffee?" I asked Jackson.

"Yes, I've heard that."

The flight attendant brought our drinks. I took a sip of mine, then told Jackson, "Well, a few Mormon families live in Cutlip, and I grew up with some of their daughters. We kids always teased them that they were refugees from Utah. Anyway, I did this obituary for a Mormon man who told everyone, including his wife, he was an IRS auditor, but he was really a marketing spy for Starbucks."

Jackson choked on his next sip. "Really?"

"Yes. Actually, it was a confession to the world. Apparently he had become addicted to something called a Grande Iced Mocha Double Caramel Tiramisu Macchiato."

"It sounds pretty amazing. Almost makes me wish I liked coffee," Jackson said.

I thumbed through my phone and found the obituary.

Darwin Strayhorn
1961–2012

Darwin Strayhorn died at the age of fifty-one after a short and difficult battle with pancreatic cancer. For several months he knew he was dying, so he requested my services. His professional life was a complete and total lie. He was not and had never been an IRS auditor. He actually hated them, like the rest of us. Who wants to talk to an IRS auditor about his job? His wife didn't even want to know about it. It was a safe cover for his real job as a Starbucks marketing spy.

Coffee is big business, which means big money, which means cut-throat competition. Drinking coffee is also against Mormon beliefs—and Darwin was and had been a Mormon his whole life. He was hired by Starbucks right out of college. It was supposed to be a temporary job, one he would keep secret until something better came along. But Darwin was good and Starbucks knew it. They threw a lot of money at him, as well as all the free coffee he could drink.

At first the idea of drinking coffee never crossed his mind, but the intoxicating aroma of roasted coffee beans began to wear on him. As months became years, his resolve weakened. He had a wife and a few kids, so the lies became bigger . . . and Darwin's hours were filled with the aroma of java. It wore on him until one day he snapped and ordered a Mini Frappuccino and downed it in one gulp. It was the most delicious thing he'd ever tasted. He drank eight more and didn't sleep for twenty-four hours.

Like most addictions, one thing led to another and before he knew it, Darwin could throw back a Grande Iced Mocha Double Caramel Tiramisu Macchiato like it was water on a hot afternoon. Each day was a mental journey of failure, beginning with a firm resolve to never drink coffee again, and ending with Darwin sitting in his darkly tented "government" vehicle, slurping the macchiato through his tears.

He wasn't a bad person, just a mortal man who gave into weakness . . . a weakness he wanted his friends and family to know and understand. He felt great relief knowing his story would be told and could become a cautionary tale for those of his faith who are tempted by the heavenly scent of coffee.

"I know this will come as a shock to my wife and family—I'm so sorry, Debbie! Hopefully the pension plan will take some of the sting out of this. You will need to talk to Antoine at the Starbucks on North Main. He has all the paperwork. He also named a drink after me, The Salted Strayhorn. I was on the cutting edge of the salted-caramel trend."

Nineteen

Jackson and I had just enough time to make our connection in New York. When we boarded the flight to Germany, we were seated in soft leather recliners with a console between us. The time change meant we took off at sunset. Once we reached cruising altitude, Jackson and I dined on grilled salmon and sautéed vegetables with real utensils. *So this is what business-class is like,* I thought *I'll never want to fly coach again.*

The flight attendant gave us blankets and pillows and said it would help with jet lag if we got some sleep. She dimmed the lights in the cabin.

"I don't think I can fall asleep so early," I told Jackson.

"She's right, though. We should try to sleep, to have a 'night' on our normal clock," he replied quietly.

"Is that what you did when you flew to New Zealand for your parents' mission?"

He smiled. "They tried to get us to settle down on the flight over, but we were too nervous and excited. That was a very long flight. This won't be anything like that."

"Where else have you traveled? I mean international flights."

He looked at me for a long moment. "I'll tell you about those trips sometime. For now, you need to rest as much as you can."

At his sad expression, it hit me that maybe he hadn't been traveling for business, as I'd assumed. *Maybe there was someone he loved . . .* But whatever his reasons, he wasn't ready to talk about it yet, so I'd need to be patient.

I reclined my seat and made myself comfortable with my pillow and blanket. Jackson did the same. When I rolled onto my side to look at him, he was lying on his side, smiling at me.

"We need to rest now. There'll be time to talk later," he said quietly. It felt like an apology for not answering my question.

He reached across the console and took my hand. He held it for a moment, rubbing his thumb across my fingers, then squeezed them and let go. I closed my eyes and tried to relax to the thrum of the engine. When I opened my eyes a few minutes later, Jackson lay on his back, staring at the ceiling.

I felt something touch me and snapped awake. Jackson was sitting up in his seat, his hand on my arm. Daylight shone through the cabin windows, and the air smelled of bacon and coffee.

"Morning, sunshine," Jackson said. I gave him half a smile and rubbed my eyes.

"You doing okay?" he asked, making me wonder what I looked like.

"Fine. Guess I slept, huh?"

He chuckled. "Yeah, you could say that. You know you snore, right?"

"No, I don't!" I retorted, frowning.

A middle-aged flight attendant came by and handed me a complimentary grooming kit. I was relieved to see she was giving them to everyone and not just those who looked like they needed it.

"She snored, huh?" he said to the flight attendant as she handed him a kit.

"Like a chainsaw." She gave a picture-perfect smile. "You practically drowned out the sound of the engine." She pointed to the front of the plane. "The bathroom is that way."

Once the flight attendant had moved on to the next passenger, I hit a very amused Jackson with my pillow, then headed to the bathroom. Inside, I locked the door and peered into the mirror. "Oh no," I gasped. My makeup was smeared, and my hair was all over the place. I looked like a wreck.

When I felt sufficiently groomed, I stepped out of the bathroom. The same flight attendant who confirmed my snoring stood just outside. She handed me a twenty-dollar bill.

"Your boyfriend gave me this to say you were snoring. I figured you were the one who deserved it."

I narrowed my eyes but smiled as she chuckled. "He really bribed you?" I asked, my mind beginning to calculate some kind of revenge on Jackson.

Grinning, the flight attendant replied, "I wouldn't be too hard on him. To see the look on his face as he watched you sleeping" —she paused and shook her head— "I'd give anything to have a man look at me like that. And you know they like you if they tease you." She winked at me.

"Oh, thanks," I said, certain I was blushing.

"By the way, several people in this cabin were snoring," confided the flight attendant. "You weren't one of them, but your boyfriend was."

I smiled. "Hmm. That's a valuable bit of information. Maybe you deserve this money."

The flight attendant shook her head. "Keep it and do something fun with him."

I thanked her again, tucked the twenty into the pocket of my tunic, and returned to my seat.

Twenty

The plane landed at Erfurt-Weimar Airport, and Jackson and I quickly made it through customs. When we walked out the front doors of the airport, I filled my lungs with the cool mid-morning air. Despite the long flight, it seemed surreal to step out into a place that looked, smelled, and sounded so different from the place we'd left.

"It feels weird, doesn't it, to be on the other side of the world?" asked Jackson.

"Yes, like we are outsiders, looking in," I said. "This must be the travel perspective everyone talks about."

He smiled and kissed me. "We'll explore this new place together and see if we can't find some dirt on Gladys."

"Sounds perfect. I can't wait to see the hotel. Didn't Markus say it's right by a river?"

"Yes, the Unstrut River. The valley is one of the most picturesque areas in all of Germany."

When the car rental place delivered our car to the curb, Jackson asked the driver for directions in German.

Impressive! The guy took a map out of his pocket and went through several instructions with Jackson, who didn't seem to struggle with the language once. The guy helped us load our luggage into the trunk, and soon we made our way out of the airport.

"Markus said the drive into Dingelstädt is beautiful," Jackson told me from behind the wheel. "It will take us about an hour."

"You told me you didn't speak much German. Sounded pretty good to me," I said, staring out at the scenery.

"I get by," Jackson responded.

I would have pushed for more information, but the landscape drew my full attention. There were fields of grass so richly green they almost looked blue. The way the breeze moved the grass reminded me of green frosting being swirled on a cake, first one way and then another.

Soon there were fields of grain, and then of cut hay, with round bales polka-dotting the fields. Quaint cottages popped up from time to time, surrounded by mowed lawns and bright flowers. The view from my window resembled a postcard. I rolled down the glass and took in the earthy smell of hay and grass as the delicious breeze ran through my hair. "It's beautiful," I shouted over the sound of the wind. I enjoyed the air for a moment longer, then rolled up my window up and turned to see Jackson grinning. We drove in silence for a few minutes before I said, "So I know you and Markus did a couple of humanitarian missions together, but how did you meet?"

"In school. His parents wanted him to attend college in the States. The guy's a brainiac with the money-math thing—really bright. You guys will have fun talking math."

Jackson paused. "Markus is one of the most solid followers of Christ I've ever met. He went with a youth group to Haiti and saw so much poverty and need that he's gone back to help several times. The service missions he and I went on together were set up by an organization called Haiti Health Initiative. They're a group of people who want to educate the people of Haiti to help them live healthier lives."

Ah, that explains some of Jackson's international flights. "That must have been quite the experience," I said. "So what was Haiti like?"

Jackson let out a long breath. "In many areas, there is a lot of suffering. The living conditions are terrible—the drinking water is filthy, there is little food, and people live in shacks made of cardboard boxes."

He didn't continue, so I asked, "What kind of aid did you give?"

"We went with a team of doctors and nurses to a small village. While the medical team taught people and saw patients, Markus and I and a few other guys helped villagers dig a well and plant some vegetable gardens. A couple men from our group taught the people better ways to farm and how to keep their water source clean. Markus and I were grunt labor, but at least we got to try to make a difference."

"Wow, that's great . . . it must be so rewarding." I thought for a moment. "So, is Markus married? Does he have a family?"

Jackson's smile seemed forced. "Yes. He married a girl he grew up with here in Germany—Ria. I've met her and she's nice. They're expecting their first baby in a few months."

"Will she be with him?" I felt as if I had to dig for information, and I wondered why Jackson wasn't more forthcoming.

"No. It will just be Markus."

Just then we passed a sign that read "Dingelstädt," and Jackson asked me to look at the map to the hotel. He seemed relieved by this turn in the conversation.

Dingelstädt was a quaint village filled with pubs and thatched-roofed shops surrounded by farmland. The river snaked through it, and I noticed many nice restaurants along the waterfront. Soon we arrived at the Reifenstein Hotel, just outside of the village. The hotel looked modern and new. We parked in front and walked through the main entrance into a lobby decorated with light blues and chrome in a minimalist style.

After Jackson had checked us in, a bellhop helped us to our rooms. The entire hotel staff spoke English—what a relief. Not that Jackson didn't enjoy using his German language every chance he got. I watched with fascination as he spoke to the man at the front desk and then the bellhop.

My beautiful room featured icy-blue carpet, bedding, and drapes, with accents in white and chrome. To my left, wall-to-ceiling windows offered an amazing view of the tree-lined river three stories below. I ran my fingers across the top of the nightstand to make sure all of this was real.

"Nice, huh?" Jackson said from behind me. I had left the door open.

"I can't believe I'm here. And yes, it's gorgeous," I replied, then turned to see him leaning against the door frame. He was watching me the way a parent watches a child open a gift, and I thought of what the flight attendant had said about my "boyfriend" watching me sleep.

On the way from the airport, Jackson and I had decided to check into the hotel and rest a while, then walk down to the riverfront to find a place to eat. We wouldn't be meeting up with Markus until morning.

"Knock on my door when you're ready to go," Jackson told me now.

I replied that I wouldn't be long, and he shut my door. Then I did a swan dive into the two feather duvets atop my bed.

Twenty-One

Taking a shower and changing my clothes went a long way to helping me feel more awake, though my inner clock still wondered if it was morning or evening.

When Jackson opened his door, I noticed his room was similar to mine, though his view was of the sloping farmlands. He looked handsome in jeans, a cream pullover, and a gray jacket. I wore a sweater, grateful for his advice to dress for cooler weather.

As we walked through the lobby, a clerk was starting a fire in a huge stone fireplace. The back of the hotel featured a large patio with several cozy conversation areas surrounding small fire pits. The setting reminded me of fall back home, except this was the end of May in Germany.

Jackson took my hand and we walked along the river path that led toward the village. "Your friend really went all out with this hotel—it's gorgeous," I said as we passed under a huge tree that draped heavily over the water's edge. "I'm definitely helping out with the cost of staying here."

"It's fine, Lizzy," Jackson replied. "I've got it covered, and I'm taking care of the food, too." At my frown, he said, "All right, you can contribute something, but let's talk about it later. Right now I want to tell you something." He pulled me under a shady tree. The branches hung so low we were partially concealed. He took my face in his hands and kissed me. His lips were warm against the cool evening air. "You're my guest on this trip. It doesn't matter what Mr. Jonas says, I wanted you to come with me because I like being with you. So let me take care of things, okay?"

I took in a deep breath—Jackson smelled amazing. I kissed him lightly and smiled. "Can I at least buy you dinner tonight? I have an extra twenty on me." He watched me take his bribe money out of my pocket. "I don't snore, by the way," I said.

Jackson looked shocked. "The flight attendant gave that back to you?"

"Yep," I replied.

"And she said you weren't snoring?"

"Yep. And she told me that *you* snore, Jackson!"

He laughed heartily, which made me like him even more. I slid the twenty-dollar bill back into my pocket.

"Okay, we'll get dessert with that," he said. "Should we go to that place over there?" He pointed to a restaurant with patio seating.

"Looks good to me." Smiling, I took his hand.

At a table lit with candles and situated next to a warm fire, Jackson and I ate a traditional German stew called *eintopf*, served with the most amazing dark bread. For dessert we shared a giant piece of Black Forest cake. The moon rose in a clear sky of stars as we ate and talked.

We were just getting ready to ask the waiter for the ticket when someone called Jackson's name. Seconds later, a thirtyish man pulled Jackson out of his chair into a hug. He slapped Jackson on the back and said, "It's been too long, my friend."

Jackson wiped his eyes and swallowed a few times. "Too long, Markus," he finally managed. I watched and wondered as they embraced again, the air thick with the emotion of these two "brothers" reuniting.

Markus pulled away and turned to me. "And this must be Elizabeth Langston." This was my first clear look at him. He stood at least as tall as Jackson and was tan with blond hair . . . and very handsome. A distinct German accent laced his perfect English.

"It's Lizzy." I held out my hand, but he pulled me into a welcoming hug.

"I am honored to finally meet you," he said as we all sat down. "I hope you don't mind me surprising you both by coming early. I got away sooner than planned and could not wait to see you. The hotel clerk said you left on foot and headed this way, so I started checking every restaurant."

Jackson cleared some of the emotion from his throat. "It's great you're here and I'm so glad you found us. It's really good to see you."

"The hotel is amazing. Thank you for arranging for our rooms—it's so beautiful," I said, wanting to give Jackson a moment to collect himself.

"Wonderful. I'm so glad you like it," Markus replied. "Shall we let them clean things up here and we will walk back? I've taken care of the check—dinner's on me tonight." Jackson and I protested, but Markus waved us off. "You are in my country now and I'm taking care of you." He gave Jackson a challenging smile.

"I know how you operate—I'll get even with you," came the reply.

"Well, we'll see," Markus countered. "And nice try with paying my hotel room. I changed that right away." He was, of course, staying at the same hotel as us.

"What did you do?" Jackson asked.

"I'm treating a dear friend and his girlfriend like I would my family, because they are family." Markus smiled victoriously.

The guys bantered back and forth for a few minutes. I sighed to myself, then slid the twenty out of my pocket and left it on the table for the waiter.

Twenty-Two

Since fires had been lit on the deck of our hotel, we made ourselves comfortable next to one, sinking into large chairs piled with cushions and blankets. Markus turned the conversation from check paying to our mission here in Germany. "I've made a few enquiries here in Dingelstädt, so I have a starting point for us tomorrow. There is a rest home that is caring for a man who lived in the village during the time your Gladys would have been here. And there is a woman—a teacher, I believe—who is still alive, whom we can see as well. I think we should start with her."

"Thank you for doing this," I told Markus. "I know you're missing time with your family to help us."

"Yes, thank you," Jackson added.

Markus smiled. "It is not a problem, my friend, I promise you. How could I pass up a chance to see you and meet the secret obituary writer of Cutlip, Montana? I would not miss it for the world." When he asked Markus for help with the case, Jackson had, with my permission, mentioned my secret job. Since he trusted Markus completely, I felt fine about the disclosure.

I chuckled, and after a pause, Markus said, "I understand that very few people know about your secret job. You can rest easy that your anonymity is safe with me. But I'm curious, how is what you write for these people different from regular obituaries?"

I told him how it all began with Loretta Campbell, Mr. Jonas, and my iPod, and then explained what it evolved into. I told Markus about some of the obituaries I'd already shared with Jackson, as well as a few new ones. They were both laughing so hard people were looking at us. When I finished telling them about Mr. de La Fosse's memorial honoring his dedication to Big Gulps, I was stifling my yawns and forcing my eyes to stay open.

Markus, Jackson, and I went upstairs together, since our rooms were on the same floor. Markus said good night and headed off down the hallway. Jackson kissed me at my door and made sure I got safely inside the room before he went to his.

Almost as soon as my head hit the crisp white pillowcase, I was out.

Firman de La Fosse
1929–2006

Firman de La Fosse died at the age of seventy-seven from a stroke during his daily ritual of walking to the 7-Eleven for a Dr. Pepper Big Gulp and a copy of the Enquirer. *The store manager found him lying on the sidewalk bathed in Dr. Pepper and still gripping his tabloid—a fitting posture according to his wife, Nettie, because "he died as he lived, clinging to his vulgar drink and lies." She contacted me because she wanted to expound on this a bit.*

Firman and Antoinette (Nettie) de La Fosse had been married for fifty-five years at the time of his death. Like all lengthy marriages, theirs was filled with "both good and bad, along with a dose of the ridiculous—a very heavy dose." Firman had a reputation for sharing a fish tale or two, but according to Nettie "He could hold his own with any gossipmonger in the county." Being a woman of mature years and sturdy stature, and having a keen interest in the world around her, Nettie felt she was often unjustly labelled a gossip when, in fact, it was Firman who deserved this title. He was so "hopped up on sugar and caffeine from drinking his beloved Dr. Pepper, he didn't know what was coming out of his mouth."

According to Nettie, Firman's habit of fizzy drinks and falsehoods was a direct result of his lack of sufficient responsibilities at church. As faithful members of the Cutlip Community Church, both Firman and Nettie had served in many capacities over the years. However, when he began helping in the church library shortly after he retired, his life took a turn for the worse. He simply had too much time on his hands. It was customary for retired men to be called to serve in the library, but apparently there were already eight serving there—a number Nettie described as a "recipe for disaster."

Apparently Firman made the most of this free time and could often be found "huddled in the corner of the library with the other librarians, trying to one-up each other with their cockamamie stories." It was this competition for the most scandalous scuttlebutt that led Firman to the magazine rack for an Enquirer *and the healing effects of Dr. Pepper. "Healing effects, my hind end!" proclaimed Nettie. "He would use it to stay awake. What man his age can stay awake during church?" It didn't take long until Firman was hooked on the bubbly sweetness of Dr. Pepper and stories about aliens, Bigfoot, and a farmer who swore he saw Elvis weeding his corn. Well-caffeinated and armed with a list of ridiculous yarns, Firman was ready. Once the Sunday school bell rang he'd gather his cronies, pass around a bag of Werther's Caramels, and hold court.*

Somehow Firman was asked to remain in the library an unprecedented six years. Nettie is sure he paid somebody off, but she doesn't want to be the source of hearsay. She would also like to thank Amir, the 7-Eleven manager, who, heartbroken at the loss of his good friend, used Big Gulp cups and outdated Enquirers *to fashion a lovely sidewalk memorial on the site of Firman's death.*

Twenty-Three

The morning was crisp, but the day promised to be sunny and mild. Jackson, Markus, and I sat outside a small bakery, devouring scrumptious strudel and washing it down with hot chocolate. Dingelstädt proper was a lovely, quaint village with A-framed shops and cobblestone streets. Each shop had a decorative sign hanging from elaborate iron arms, and Jackson translated the words for me. There was a bookstore, a clothing boutique, a jeweler, and many restaurants and bakeries. From each lamppost hung huge flower baskets overflowing with pinks and yellows and purples. Each window box featured the same. I could smell the blooms' spicy-sweet fragrance from where I sat.

I had slept coma-like from the effects of jet lag, but got up before sunrise feeling fairly awake. Markus and Jackson had stayed up late talking.

"Let's start with Rita Schulz," Markus was saying now. "I found out she lives with family not far from here.

When Gladys was a child, Rita taught at the only school in Dingelstädt. I think she is our best chance to learn more about Gladys Ziggler's family."

"Yes, that sounds good," I said, silently wondering if Rita Schulz would remember anything about Gladys and her family from so long ago.

"If my dates are correct, Gladys came to America when she was about fifteen," Jackson put in. "So she must have attended school here."

After breakfast, we drove a short distance beyond the village and turned onto a dirt road lined with small, well-kept homes. Markus parked in front of a home with a thatched roof, trimmed lawn, and window boxes overflowing with blossoms. We got out and walked to the front door. Before we could knock, the door flew open, revealing a tall, pretty, slender young woman with blond hair pulled back in a bun. She wore all black and had obviously been crying. She stared at us with a hesitant expression, as if she had been expecting someone else.

Speaking in German, Markus introduced himself, along with Jackson and me, to the girl. Then she and Markus conversed, with Jackson interjecting an occasional comment. Soon, Markus took the young woman's hands in his and expressed what appeared to be warm condolences.

The mood was heavy when Markus, Jackson, and I got back into the SUV. "Rita passed away a few days ago," Markus announced to catch me up. "The girl was her granddaughter, who cared for her. She was on her way to help plan the funeral."

Jackson let out a long breath. "Not such great timing on our parts, huh?"

"She obviously loved her grandmother very much," I said, sorry for the girl and equally sorry we didn't have an opportunity to chat with Rita.

"I did ask her if her grandmother ever mentioned a Braun family in the area. She said no," Markus explained. He glanced at Jackson and then back at me. "I am sorry this did not work out, but we still have Alfred Schmidt to see. The rest home where he lives is about an hour away."

As we drove, Markus explained that Alfred Schmidt had lived his entire life in Dingelstädt and probably knew just about everyone. He was a carpenter by trade so would have worked on many homes in the area, so perhaps he at least knew Gladys's family.

For several miles, we continued along the road in silence. I assumed that like me, Jackson realized we might actually go home empty-handed. Not wanting to give space to these doubtful thoughts, I began telling Markus more about our Zumba-loving ladies. Jackson pitched in where he could. We talked about Betty Whipple and her pampered dog, Stella Perkins and her bitterness toward tractors, and Doris Peet's cat hoarding. Madge Abernathy's image issues came up in the conversation, but the urban legends surrounding Geraldine Nesbitt's preference for dating younger men filled several miles with interesting discussion. And, of course, the details of Mr. Jonas's first Zumba class had us all laughing.

Before we knew it, Markus was parking the SUV in front of a large rest home. At the front desk he introduced us and asked if we might see Alfred Schmidt. A lengthy exchange took place between Markus and the receptionist. When she walked away from the desk, Markus told me that Mr. Schmidt did not accept visitors other than family members, but that after some persuasion the receptionist had agreed to ask him if he would give us a few moments of his time. She had invited us to wait in the small sitting area in the lobby.

The massive building had obviously been a family residence before it was transformed into a nursing home. I could see down a long hall lined with several doorways to what had probably been bedrooms and now served as patient rooms. Where we sat seemed to have been a parlor or music room. The other direction looked to be a great room that led to a spacious kitchen. The lovely place felt comfortable and homey, but the longer we waited the more nervous I got that we might hit another dead end.

After several minutes the receptionist returned with news. Mr. Schmidt would see us after his lunch and nap. Could we come back in an hour and a half? Markus cheerfully agreed, and he and Jackson and I headed off to get some food.

Twenty-Four

At a restaurant not far from the rest home, we sat at a comfortable booth by a large window. Markus ordered meat sandwiches and delicious potato pancakes for us. German food hadn't been on my radar before this trip, but I was fast becoming a fan.

Although Mr. Schmidt was the last of Markus's two contacts, he assured us he had a few more tricks up his sleeve in the form of little-known church records. I hoped it didn't come to us spending several days going through old papers, but I was willing to do it if it was all we had. I prayed Mr. Schmidt would remember something about the Braun family.

When the conversation turned to school, Markus asked me about my math degree and teaching. Clearly the guy loved numbers. After several minutes, though, I changed the subject with "Tell me more about these humanitarian missions you two went on. I've thought of doing something like that."

The mood turned heavy as Markus and Jackson exchanged glances. "You served together in Haiti, right?" I asked Markus.

After a noticeable pause, he replied, "Yes. The missions were amazing. I highly recommend you go on one." Markus explained a little about the humanitarian organization he and Jackson had served with. Jackson sat in silence.

Suddenly, Markus looked at him and said, "Did you tell Lizzy about any of the people we met there?"

Jackson shot him an angry look, then stood and said, "Can we talk about this later? We need to go."

In silence, Markus and I followed him to the front of the restaurant. As Jackson paid the bill, I gave Markus a concerned look, but he just shrugged and shook his head.

Wow, what's going on here? What happened in Haiti that has Jackson so upset? Whatever it was, he clearly didn't want to talk about it and felt it wasn't Markus's place to tell me. I resolved to be patient, but my imagination started kicking in bigtime.

Back at the nursing home, the receptionist greeted us and led us down the hallway. Earlier, she had explained that Mr. Schmidt had dementia, but as we entered his room now she whispered that this was a good day for him. He sat in a chair next to a window. He had bright-blue eyes and a full head of gray hair. His hands still showed the signs of being the main tools of his carpentry trade. With a guarded smile he greeted us.

Markus shook Mr. Schmidt's hand and introduced the three of us. The elderly gentleman nodded to Markus, and then to Jackson and me, and uttered a greeting in German. Someone, I'm assuming the receptionist, had placed three chairs in the room. Markus and Jackson spoke to Mr. Schmidt, occasionally translating the exchange to English for me.

A couple of times during their conversation in German, I glanced around the room and out at people walking by the door. Several nurses and aides passed by, some carrying trays of food or piles of neatly folded linens. I couldn't help but notice one girl hovering around the door, trying to appear busy but probably listening to every word that was said. Perhaps mysterious American visitors would be a hot topic for the staff, and the girl wanted to be the one in the know.

As I focused on the conversation once more, Markus mentioned the name Gladys Braun. Until that point in the exchange, Mr. Schmidt had worn a pleasant expression and seemed to readily answer the questions posed by Markus and Jackson. But as soon as Markus uttered Gladys's name, Alfred Schmidt's eyes turned dark and his lips pressed into a straight line. He shook his head and spoke in a harsh tone. When both Markus and Jackson tried some gentle encouragement, he shook his head again, this time violently. Through gritted teeth he uttered something that caused Markus and Jackson to stare at each other in shock. Then Mr. Schmidt pushed a button on the table next to his chair.

Almost immediately, the receptionist stormed in and ordered us to leave. Markus thanked Mr. Schmidt, who waved us off abruptly. As the first person out of the room, I almost collided with the girl I'd noticed hovering just beyond the doorway. Our eyes met and I gave her a knowing smile. Her cheeks flushed and her gaze darted to the floor before she hurried off.

Markus, Jackson, and I climbed into the SUV and sat in silence for a moment. "That was weird," said Markus finally, more to himself than to us.

Jackson sighed his agreement. "Lizzy, I'm sure we missed translating some of what we talked about in there, so I'll just tell you all of it to cover everything. Mr. Schmidt, who we already knew was a carpenter, was well acquainted with almost all the families in the area. He seemed to enjoy telling me about a few families he knew were still living in Dingelstädt. But when we mentioned Gladys and the Braun family, he became agitated and angry. He said they were evil and then refused to speak of them again."

"Why do you think he'd act that way?" I asked right before it hit me. *This is Nazi Germany we're talking about.*

"My best guess? The Braun family played some kind of role in the war—apparently not a very popular role," Jackson replied. This seemed to confirm what Gladys said in the note she left on my door.

We took a moment to absorb this possibility, and then Markus explained, "Since Gladys's family lived here, there has to be something or someone in the area that can tell us more. I had hoped it wouldn't come to this, but it looks like we'll need to do some record searching. I have a friend who can get us into the church archives at the township office. They will be closed by the time we get back, so we should plan an early start tomorrow."

"So we just start looking through random records?" I asked, overwhelmed.

"Exactly. We will be able to narrow it a bit, but yes, that is what we will need to do." Markus must have seen the panic on my face, because he added. "Don't worry, my friend. We will find something sooner than you think."

"How can you know that?" I asked.

"You have to have faith," Jackson and Markus replied in unison. They looked at each other in surprise and began to laugh.

I smiled as I watched them, their eyes shining, and wondered if this had to do with Haiti too.

Markus started the SUV, and Jackson said, "Let's drive back to the hotel and call it a day."

Twenty-Five

Markus pulled up in front of the hotel to drop us off. Ria, his wife, had asked him to pick up a few items at a shop in the village. He put the SUV in park and turned to face Jackson and me. I was in the front passenger seat, and Jackson sat behind me in the back.

"I will probably be a while," Markus said. "Let's plan on leaving around eight in the morning." We voiced our agreement and thanked him again. Then Markus looked directly at Jackson and said, "Brother, you need to tell her—tonight." I had suspected Markus wanted to give us some alone time, and now I felt certain of it.

Jackson said nothing, but I turned just in time to see his slight nod to his friend. As I opened my door and got out, my insides screamed, *Tell me what?* If Jackson didn't fill me in soon, I would explode. It wouldn't be pretty.

"Let's walk by the river." He held out his hand to me.

I took it and let him pull me up and into his arms. I buried my face in his neck and whispered, "You okay?"

"Not really." He kissed the top of my head and moved back a little. His eyes held mine for a second, and then he smiled, but only with his mouth.

We walked down by the river, the late-afternoon sun starting to cast shadows. Jackson grabbed a couple of lawn chairs the hotel had set out for guests to use. He led me under a shady tree, then positioned the chairs close together, so we would be facing each other. Once we were seated, I took his hand and held it against my cheek. He leaned in and kissed me softly.

"I need to tell you some things about my past, about Haiti." His lips brushed the words against my mouth.

"Okay," I answered.

Jackson kissed me again and leaned back in his chair, his fingers woven through mine. "On our first mission to Haiti, Markus and I met the Jean-Pierre family," he began. "They were poor, living on next to nothing in a small village, but their Christian faith was strong. 'You have to have faith' was their family motto."

I smiled, now understanding why Markus and Jackson had said that together.

"We helped them as much as we could," Jackson continued, "and before we left I gave them all the money, extra clothes, and food I had with me. They were wonderful, warm people. I became friends with their oldest daughter, Leila, and gave her my address. Writing actual letters would be the only way she could afford to communicate with me.

"We wrote back and forth and even managed to talk on the phone a few times. When Markus and I returned to Haiti the following year, I spent more time with Leila. She was a beautiful person, and I fell in love with her."

Jackson stopped to swallow a few times, his eyes shining. "We talked about marriage, so when I got back to the United States, I started the paperwork to sponsor her and eventually her family. We knew it would be difficult and that some people would only see an American man marrying a poor Haitian woman. But Leila and I didn't care about that. We loved each other. We planned a life together, and we dreamed of a better life for her family. Then it happened . . . on January 12, 2010." Jackson paused, his cheeks wet with tears.

I shut my eyes for a moment as realization flooded over me. "The earthquake," I whispered.

Jackson wiped his face and nodded. "Leila and her entire family died. Somehow I made it to Haiti. With chaos everywhere, I hoped there had been a mistake—that she was still alive. Markus met me there and we searched for days. Finally, we found their bodies." Jackson paused before closing his eyes and saying quietly, "They had died together—Leila wasn't alone." He paused again as we both cried. I reached up and wiped away his tears.

"There was no one to bury them." Jackson's voice caught, and he had to clear his throat before going on. "So we took their bodies to a spot where Leila and I would walk sometimes. Markus and I dug graves for her and her family, and after the burial he stood with me as I prayed over each one. I couldn't have done it without him.

"We stayed in Haiti and helped as long as we could, but then we had to come back. Life went on—school and work and family—but I was angry. I just kind of shut down for a while, and even quit attending church. It felt as if I had lost my faith." Jackson took a few deep breaths.

"Markus and my family were a great support to me. I threw myself into my work. I discovered that the more I helped people, the less anger I felt. I came back to church and to the Lord, who took me in with open arms. But even after all of that, I still believed I would never feel anything for a woman again." Jackson shook his head a little, a grin spreading over his face. "And then I agreed to help an old friend and met a beautiful woman who writes secret obituaries."

Twenty-Six

I smiled back at Jackson, relief washing over me. "You have feelings for me and you feel guilty."

He closed his eyes for a few seconds, then opened them and replied, "You don't deserve to be with a guy who's so messed up."

"You're not messed up—you're human," I told him gently. "I might be young and inexperienced in many ways, but writing those obituaries has taught me a few things." I stopped, trying to put my thoughts into words. "The experiences we've had, both good and bad, make us who we are today. If you love someone, you don't want to change who that person has become. In other words, you wouldn't wish away any of their experiences."

Jackson furrowed his brow, clearly wondering where I was going with this.

I put my hands on his shoulders. "I'm so sorry you had to go through what you did, losing Leila, and in such a tragic way. But I'm not sorry that you loved her."

"You don't feel threatened by my memories of another woman—someone I wanted to marry?"

"Of course not. She must have been a very special girl, because loving her has made you a man I like and admire very much. I don't know why she was taken from you, but I trust that God has a perfect plan and all will be right in the end."

Jackson looked at me for a long moment. "You are a wise woman, Elizabeth Langston," he said, a hesitant grin turning up the corners of his mouth.

"I don't know about wise, but I do know that if we allow Him, the Lord can make our hearts love in a much greater capacity than we ever imagined. There should always be a place in your heart for Leila, and that's okay. In fact, it makes me even more attracted to you, knowing you have loved someone so deeply."

Jackson chuckled. "So the guy you're dating starts acting strange and won't talk about some stuff, then drops the bomb that he almost married a Haitian girl who died, and that he is still dealing with that and all kinds of guilt. You're really okay with that?"

"I am, because I understand you now. That's another thing I've learned from my secret job. It's so much better when we give other people a chance to understand us. It's the unknown, the not understanding, that messes everything up. Now that I know what you're going through, I can help you, even just by listening. I can be a shoulder to cry on, if you need that, and help share some of your burden."

"Like in the Bible where we are told to 'weep with them that weep,'" Jackson replied.

"Yes, that's exactly what I mean."

He looked at me for another long moment. "Thank you, Lizzy. Thank you for this. I feel . . . better."

Smiling, I offered a silent prayer of gratitude for my job as the secret obituary writer. It had definitely taught me to look at life from a different perspective.

Jackson and I ate dinner under the stars, talking and laughing. For the first time, I felt as if I was seeing the real man.

Twenty-Seven

The next morning, Markus and I made it down to the lobby before Jackson did. When Markus asked if I was okay, I smiled and said I was doing great. Just then, Jackson walked up beside me. The two friends exchanged some nonverbal communication, and Markus was visibly relieved. Everyone seemed in a brighter mood as we drove to the records office.

An overwhelming number of boxes stuffed with town records greeted us. I opened one box, sending a million particles of dust into the air. The morning light from the window seemed to make them dance. "Once we isolate the boxes dated within the time frame we're looking for, we'll start going through the records inside," Markus reminded me. I shut my box, sending more dust into the air. Markus showed me the markings on the box and what to look for, so we could set aside those from Gladys's time in Dingelstädt.

We worked in comfortable silence for a while, Jackson catching my eye and touching my shoulder as he'd pass me. By noon the three of us had isolated a large stack of boxes to be searched. Having eaten a quick breakfast on the way to the office, we decided to get some lunch before attacking the contents of the boxes. Markus wanted to take us to a certain restaurant we had passed on the way to the rest home the day before, and although it was a little drive, Jackson and I were happy for the break. The restaurant had a beautiful patio area, but since the day was cool we ate inside. We stuffed ourselves with roast and potatoes and vegetables—all delicious.

As we were getting ready to leave, someone by the door waved at us. I moved closer and realized it was the young girl from the rest home—the girl I suspected of eavesdropping on us. She wasn't dressed in her uniform from the home, so I didn't immediately recognize her. When we made eye contact, she smiled and waved me over to her. "I'm sorry to interrupt your lunch, but I'm so happy to have found you," she said in heavily accented English.

"You're the girl from the nursing home. I saw you outside Mr. Schmidt's room, right?"

"Yes. I know it was wrong, but when I heard your friend mention the Braun family, I stayed close to hear what they were asking."

"Do you know the Braun family?" I asked. Markus and Jackson had caught up with me by that point.

"My grandfather does," the girl responded. "He was a teacher at the school and taught Gladys and her friend, Jacob Ziggler."

I stared in happy disbelief.

"You know Gladys Braun *and* Jacob Ziggler?" Jackson asked in surprise.

"I don't, but my grandfather does," the girl said. "You will need to talk to him. If you would like, I can take you to see him. He lives with us. It is not too far from here—we can walk."

Jackson and I could hardly contain our excitement, and we got a few stares for it.

As we walked, the girl introduced herself as Eva Herrman. She said her grandfather, Hans Herrman, had taught music and dance at the only school in Dingelstädt. Gladys had been one of his favorite students.

We turned down a street lined with larger homes and nice-sized lawns. Eva stopped at the second house on the right and said, "Before we go in, you need to know that my grandfather is blind. He lost his sight a few years ago, which is why he's living with us. Otherwise, he's perfectly healthy. His mind is as sharp as a . . . tack?"

We laughed. Markus, speaking in German, gave her what seemed to be a compliment.

The Herrman home was very nice and spacious, with rambling lawns, and a roofline with three brick chimneys. Eva explained that her family was away for the day and she had stayed to look after her grandfather. She had walked over to the restaurant to buy his daily dose of *splitterbrotchen*—a popular German pastry. She had called the hotel number we had left at the nursing home, but the deskman had informed her that we were out for the day. It was a stroke of luck she had chanced upon us in the village.

In Eva's house, I felt my first real pang of homesickness since the flight to Germany. The beautifully decorated home seemed to have been lovingly lived in. Eva guided us through a front parlor and into a large kitchen. The kitchen proper was at one end of the rectangular room, and a large fireplace stood at the other end. The opposite wall consisted of large windows looking out on a beautiful lawn surrounded by trees. I imagined this was a cozy gathering place for the family during the long winters.

In an easy chair next to the fireplace, an elderly man sat, snoring softly. When we entered the room, Eva smiled and whispered, "My grandfather speaks English and will enjoy talking to you."

"Will he be alarmed when he wakes up to three American strangers wanting to talk to him?" I asked.

Eva smiled and shook her head. "This is exactly the sort of thing my grandfather loves."

We moved closer to the hearth. Broad shoulders hinted of Hans Herrman's past strength, though he sat somewhat hunched with age. He was bald, the only hair on his head being a pair of bushy eyebrows. His hands, with the fingers of a pianist, were folded gracefully on his lap.

Eva gently rubbed her grandfather's arm. His eyes flew open but stared straight ahead, sightless. His face filled with a smile as he patted her hand. They conversed in German, and then Hans Herrman's face lit up, his eyebrows dancing. "Eva, my dear, you got me three Americans on whom I can try my English, and I didn't get you anything," he said with a strong German accent. We all chuckled. "Welcome, welcome," he told us. "Please shake my hand and tell me your names again, so I can see you. I'm sure my Eva has explained that I can no longer see with my eyes."

"She has." I reached out and took his hand. "Thank you for allowing us to interrupt your nap. My name is Elizabeth Langston, but everyone calls me Lizzy."

Still smiling, the elderly man wrapped his long fingers around my hand. "Lizzy—I like that." He gave my hand a pat before letting go.

He made similar introductions with Jackson and Markus. Eva brought over three chairs and motioned for us to sit down. When she began to stir the fire to life, Jackson and Markus each added a log from a nearby stack. I felt the increase of warmth as the blaze took hold.

"Grandfather, my new friends have questions about the Braun family, about Gladys Braun," Eva said.

Hans's eyes lit up despite his blindness. "My little Gladys! You know of her?"

"Yes. She lives in my town," I answered.

"And Jacob? Jacob Ziggler?"

I paused, realizing Mr. Herrman probably knew nothing of either of them after they escaped Germany. "Yes, they both made it to America," I said. "They married and raised a family. Jacob passed away a few years ago, but Gladys is doing well. They were very happy."

Tears streamed down Hans's face. He took a neatly folded handkerchief from his pocket and wiped away the moisture. "I prayed so many times that the Nazis never found them," he mumbled.

"Could you tell us a little about Gladys and her family? The newspaper I work for is doing a special tribute to World War II survivors as a surprise. There's not much information about the Braun family—in fact, it's as if they never existed." Mr. Jonas really planned to do the tribute, which I was excited about.

"You won't find anything about them, and there's a very good reason why," Hans declared.

Twenty-Eight

"You are speaking to one of very few people who will tell you anything about the Braun family," Hans continued. Then his voice turned sad. "Though almost everyone else who knew them is dead."

"Are you comfortable talking about this?" asked Jackson.

"Of course, especially now that I am certain Gladys and Jacob survived. However, I do not think she will want all of this in the newspaper. I will tell you about her family, but you must promise to seek her approval before printing any of it. It will ruin the surprise, but much of what I am going to share is not pleasant. I hope Gladys has made peace with it by now."

"I promise we'll get her approval," I said.

Hans began, "At the time of the war, Dingelstädt was a small village. Everyone knew each other. Gladys was the youngest child and only girl in the Braun family. She had several older brothers. I taught music and dance at the school. I was not much older than my students." The elderly man chuckled. "Gladys was a natural. She was one of my most eager students, always happy and so alive. She had a creative drive I had never seen before in one so young,"

Markus said something in German that caused Hans to nod in agreement. "It's a German expression meaning she has a gift from God," Markus explained to me.

"That was my little Gladys," Hans went on. "But when the war broke out, it changed everything. It took the life out of everyone—even one as gifted as Gladys." He paused for a moment and we remained silent, allowing him space to unfold the story.

"One thing the war could not take was the love between Gladys and Jacob. But Jacob Ziggler and his family were Jewish, and the Brauns, all but Gladys, were Nazis." Hans paused as if to allow this news to sink in. "Gladys's parents strictly forbid her to even speak to Jacob, and when she refused to end the romance, her father, a Nazi officer, ordered Jacob's death. That is when Gladys and Jacob came to me. You see, I secretly helped many Jews escape to America."

"Like the Underground Railroad," I said softly.

"Yes, very much like your Underground Railroad that helped the slaves," Hans said. "I am very thankful that Gladys and Jacob made it. She had to cut off all ties to her family and friends, even me. She did what she needed to do to protect Jacob and herself."

Things were starting to fall into place. Gladys didn't want anyone snooping around her studio—and her life—if there was even a remote chance of uncovering this.

"Gladys's father ordered the deaths of many Jewish families in the area. Gladys and Jacob's escape humiliated and infuriated him."

Remembering Gladys's threat about her family not hesitating to kill made me wince.

"The Nazis hunted for Gladys and Jacob for several years, but I made sure their tracks were covered. I knew they had made it to America, but like I said, all connections had to be severed for their safety. To finally find out that they were never found and had a happy life fills me with joy." Knowing how well Hans Herrman had done his job made me look at him with new eyes. I wondered what powerful and far-reaching connections this grandfather once had.

"Have you spoken with anyone else in the area?" Hans asked us.

Markus and I briefly explained our poor timing with Rita Schulz, and the angry response from Alfred Schmidt.

Hans sighed. "I am afraid if Rita had lived long enough to meet you, her response would have been much the same. The Brauns ordered the deaths of people Rita and Alfred both loved."

We sat in silence for a moment, the air heavy with an unspoken question.

"You are wondering if they ordered the deaths of someone I loved. The answer is yes," Hans said quietly.

"How did you live through that?" The words flew out of my mouth before I could stop them. I wanted to ask this of anyone who survived the Holocaust. But Hans Herrman didn't just survive it—he appeared to thrive, living a life rich with love and family.

"My dear, I chose to love instead of hate. It's as simple as that." His voice was thick with emotion. "And I took that love and helped people like Gladys and Jacob make their way to freedom."

"The names of all the people Grandfather helped escape are written in our family Bible," Eva explained. "There are 208 names."

"That's amazing," I said under my breath.

"I will tell you what is amazing," Hans replied. "The human heart. It was created to love, not to hate."

I glanced at Jackson and smiled.

"My life has been happy because I chose to love. I had plenty of reasons to close my heart and hate. This life gives just about every person a reason to hate, but it also gives us many opportunities to love."

"I couldn't agree with you more," Jackson said, his eyes shining in the firelight. The room had darkened, and I noticed towering gray clouds through the window.

"We've taken enough of your time," I said, coming to my feet. Jackson and Markus stood as well.

"You are more than welcome to stay and wait out the storm. We would love to have you visit as long as you like," Eva said.

As much as I wanted to curl up in front of the fire and hear all about Hans Herrman's fascinating life, we simply did not have time. So, I reached down and took his hand, saying, "We really should be going."

"I loved meeting you, Lizzy. Perhaps you'll tell my little Gladys to call me?"

"I will, Mr. Herrman. I am certain she'll be very happy to speak with you after all these years."

Jackson and Markus said their goodbyes after we quickly exchanged contact information with Eva. The three of us dashed back to the village and barely made it to the SUV before the skies opened up.

Twenty-Nine

"When you told me what you were looking for, I feared you might find this," Markus admitted. "Though the war happened decades ago, it still effects many lives—and will for generations." Rain pounded so loudly on the windows that he had to raise his voice so Jackson and I could hear him. We sat in the SUV waiting out the storm.

"I can't imagine having your father order the death of the man you love," I said.

Markus sighed. "And the deaths of neighbors both she and Jacob probably knew and loved."

"I want to hear how he helped all those people," Jackson said, more to himself than to us.

We talked for a few more minutes as rain continued to pour. When it died down to a drizzle, Markus started the engine and we returned to the records department. We no longer needed the contents of the dusty boxes, though I was sure they held many secrets. It took us about an hour to get things in order again.

Back at the hotel, Jackson and I made arrangements to fly home in the morning. After he and Markus worked out a compromise with the hotel bill, they spoke quietly to each other for a moment and then shared a quick hug. Markus embraced me and said he hoped we would meet again.

The afternoon rain had left a clear, clean sky. Jackson and I curled up in front of a fire on the patio, with thick blankets draped across our laps. The air was wet with the smell of earth and flowers. We sat in comfortable silence, each deep in our own thoughts.

"I'm glad I met Mr. Herrman," Jackson finally said. "I'm glad we found out what we needed for Gladys and all that, but I needed to meet Hans." He paused for a moment, then explained. "After I lost Leila I was angry—really angry. It consumed me and changed how I did everything. My whole life I'd been taught that God is a loving God, but that since we are mortal and live in a fallen world, bad things happen to good people. But once pain became my reality, I wondered if I trusted God, or even loved Him anymore. How could I, when he had let something so terrible happen to me, and to Leila and her family?

"I threw myself into my work and found that serving people made me forget about the pain a little. I know this sounds corny, but because of that there was more room in my heart to feel God's love. It seems like Hans did the same, though it's hard to imagine how much he suffered."

"His service saved him," I said, and Jackson nodded. "So what happens when we get home?" I asked. "Will you have to call Gladys in for questioning?"

"We'll have to call all the women in, but I'll speak with her privately first. We'll have to get statements from all of them. It doesn't change that Oliver died or how he died, but his family will need to know this."

"Telling them won't be fun," I said.

"It won't, but this sort of thing is a part of my job. Hopefully whatever the judge decides will satisfy the family. As for the ladies, considering their age, and with the county jail at capacity, they'll probably just get community service. Gladys threatened you, so the judge might want to put her in jail for a little bit to teach her a lesson, but my guess is it would only be a few weeks. If she's lucky, she'll just get probation." Jackson shook his head in amusement. "At least we don't have to worry about the local newspaper printing the story. If the media found out, it could've gone viral and ended up in the national news."

"Yep. Not something we want splashed all over the front page," I said with a smile.

Thirty

I watched them through the two-way mirror—Betty, Stella, Doris, Madge, Geraldine, and Gladys. Just like the police dramas on television, I could see the suspects, but they couldn't see me. The women seemed nervous except Gladys, who appeared completely calm, having privately spoken with Jackson before this group meeting. Doris started to whimper.

"Why are we in here, being questioned about Ollie's death, when we all promised to not say anything?" demanded Stella.

"Because I told the obituary writer that Ollie didn't die by his tractor, that's why," Doris admitted between sobs.

After producing a package of pink-and-white-striped tissues and handing one to Doris, Betty said sheepishly, "I told the obituary writer, too. Guilt gives me indigestion."

Glaring at everyone, Madge sat with her legs crossed and her arms folded. Geraldine kept reapplying lipstick.

"Every one of you told the obituary writer, didn't you?" asked Gladys, her German accent more distinct than usual.

All eyes diverted to the ground as heads nodded.

Geraldine blotted her lips. "Well, I'll tell you one thing, I'd like to get my hands on that obituary writer."

Betty muffled a burp, retrieved a massive bottle of Tums out of her purse, and put three into her mouth.

"The truth is we didn't kill Ollie—a heart attack did," Gladys huffed. "It will all be fine."

Jackson entered the observation room and stood next to me, looking through the glass. "How's it going in there?"

"Oh, they're about to implode," I answered.

"Perfect. That's my cue." Jackson gave my arm a squeeze and then walked around to enter the interrogation room from the main door. He sat across the table from the women, who had arranged their chairs in a half circle. All six ladies stared at Jackson, who said, "I understand that Oliver Moore died of a heart attack while attending your Zumba class. That's why you're here, to tell me the details of that evening. We just want to know what happened."

After several seconds of silence, Stella said, "You're going to make us cancel Zumba class, aren't you?"

The room erupted in outrage.

"Quiet, please!" Jackson shouted over the noise. "We'll talk about that later." From his body language, I could tell he was holding back laughter. But when the ladies quieted, he managed to ask in a serious tone, "Who can tell me what happened that evening?"

All eyes turned to Gladys. "Well, I finally got Ollie to come to a class," she said after a pause. "He looked fine through the warm-up and the swing-and-go, but halfway through salsa and samba he just collapsed. We hoped he had fainted, but I think he was dead before he hit the floor."

"All my medical training, and I couldn't do anything. I should have done something," Doris sobbed. Betty handed over the entire package of tissues and patted her arm.

Jackson cleared his throat. "According to the autopsy report, Mrs. Ziggler is right. Oliver had a massive heart attack that killed him within seconds. No one could have done anything to save him. But why didn't you call 9-1-1? You must have realized the police needed to be notified."

"Because we didn't want our Zumba class cancelled," said one of the women. The others voiced their agreement.

I gasped, and though I couldn't see Jackson's face, I imagined his eyebrows going up in that cute way they do.

"We panicked," Gladys went on. "We knew they would be performing all kinds of inspections that would force us to shut down the studio for weeks and mess up our Zumba schedule."

"It was my idea to move his body to his tractor," Stella put in. "He spent so much time on it, no one would question him dying on the thing. So we loaded him into the back of Madge's Escalade and drove him out to his farm."

"And if we were going to all this trouble, we needed to get him in his farming clothes," Geraldine added.

"You just got tired of undressing him with your eyes and wanted to do it for real," said Betty.

"I'll have you know I did not look once," Doris exclaimed through sobs.

"This is shameful. I can't believe I went along with it," Madge muttered under her breath.

Geraldine huffed. "Madge, you went along with it because if you don't do your Zumba every week, your rear end won't fit through the door." Madge glared at her.

"So you decided to change Mr. Moore's clothes?" Jackson asked, then got up and walked around to lean against the front of the table.

"Thankfully his back door was unlocked," Gladys said. "We carried him into his mudroom. Geraldine undressed him while the rest of us looked for his work clothes."

Gladys smiled. "He kept a tight ship. Found them in no time flat. We dressed him and carried him out to his field where he had parked his tractor. We propped him up next to it and left. And thanks to the Zumba, we didn't have a problem lifting him."

All six ladies smiled and nodded proudly.

Jackson asked what time class had started, then approximately what time Mr. Moore collapsed. Later he told me that the women's responses coincided with the approximated time of death on the autopsy report.

"Because it's against the law to move a body and stage a death, there will be legal consequences," Jackson informed the suspects. "I've spoken with the county attorney, and considering your ages, the judge will probably give you community service. In fact, from what he told the attorney, you may be helping Ned Wheeler keep the cemetery looking nice. The officer outside this door will take you to fill out some paperwork, and in a few weeks you'll appear at a brief hearing. But before I let you go, will you make me a promise to call 9-1-1 if anything like this happens again?"

The ladies nodded and smiled.

"So who is this mysterious obituary writer who tattled on us?" asked Geraldine.

The women looked to Jackson, who folded his arms and said matter-of-factly, "He or she will remain anonymous.

But the writer did the correct thing by reporting the situation to the police. Now you're all free to go, except Gladys." Jackson turned to her. "I need you to stay for a bit."

The other five women filed out the door, Betty gently guiding Doris, who was still crying. As Geraldine walked passed Jackson, she leaned in close to his ear and purred, "Maybe you're the mysterious obituary writer." She squeezed his arm and batted her eyelashes before she flounced out the door.

Jackson glanced toward the two-way mirror and raised his eyebrows. Then he talked to Gladys a bit more about the judge giving her probation instead of jail time for her threatening note. He took his time, and I knew he was making sure the other women left the building without seeing me. When he was done, he tapped on the glass and smiled, our signal that I could come in.

Gladys watched as I entered the room and sat in a chair across the table from her. She immediately took hold of both my hands, her eyes filling with tears. "I am sorry I tried to scare you."

"I know." I squeezed her hands.

"The nice detective told me you both went to Germany. You spoke to Hans, yes?"

I nodded.

Tears spilled down Gladys's face. "He told you about my family? You know what my father did?"

"Yes. We learned that your parents held very different beliefs than you, and that to stay true to what and whom you loved, you came to America."

Gladys couldn't speak for a moment—she closed her eyes as more tears came. I handed her some tissues from my purse. She wiped her eyes and continued. "I was desperate. If there was a police investigation they would find out. Everyone would know my parents were Nazis, and they wouldn't believe I wasn't part of it, even though I ran away to prevent my father from killing the man I love. I will do anything to keep this from getting out."

"No one knows about it but Jackson, Markus, Mr. Jonas, and me, and we won't tell a soul. I'm very good at keeping secrets." I grinned.

"That is right. Loretta would be so proud of you," Gladys's eyes crinkled up as she smiled.

"Mrs. Campbell? You knew Loretta Campbell?" I asked shocked.

"Yes, we were dear friends. We had much in common with what we each suffered from the war." Gladys explained how she had met Loretta during a war-effort service project. The two women had remained close through the years. Loretta had told Gladys about my special visits and how much they meant to her. When Loretta felt her life was coming to a close, she told Gladys she planned to ask me to write a special obituary so others could understand who she was. She also asked Gladys to watch out for me.

"She wanted to make sure you were happy," Gladys said. "She prayed every day that you would have the courage to follow your heart. She didn't want you to suffer the unhappiness she had."

Tears blurred my eyes as I cried, missing my friend.

"I have many good friends here," Gladys went on. "Ollie and Nedra were one of the first couples to welcome Jacob and me to this area. We've been good friends for years. When Nedra became sick, I helped care for her. She asked Jacob and me to watch out for Ollie after she passed." Gladys paused for a moment as more tears ran down her cheeks. "After I lost my Jacob, Ollie checked on me every day for weeks. We would go to lunch every now and then, just as friends. When he told me he had been feeling sluggish, I talked him into coming to Zumba, thinking it would help him. Guess it didn't." Gladys chuckled sadly. "But he's with his Nedra now and that is good."

"Good friends are blessings, aren't they?" I said. "And there is a dear man in Germany who has wanted to hear from his 'little Gladys' for a very long time."

Gladys's face broke into a smile. "I cannot believe you spoke with Hans! Oh yes, I will call him—I owe him so much. And speaking of good friends, did you know I do all my shopping at Walmart? Sometimes because of my work schedule I have to shop later at night. And I notice what goes on in the parking lot." Gladys laughed as realization crossed my face. "He's a handsome young man, your Jackson. I think Loretta would approve."

Just then Jackson entered the room, and we told Gladys about our trip in detail. She clearly enjoyed hearing it, and although the thought of returning to Germany still frightened her, she desperately wanted to see Hans Herrman one more time.

"Perhaps it will help to talk to someone who understands." Gladys paused. "Lizzy, could we talk on occasion?"

After a glance at Jackson, I told Gladys I knew what she meant and would be happy to chat with her anytime.

Thirty-One

I heard a few muffles and grunts, then something that sounded like a swear word, but considering the circumstances, I let it go. The laptop screen was blank, then jumbled, and then Mr. Jonas's truck dashboard came into view. Jackson had parked his car a few blocks from the dance studio. I sat in the front passenger seat. Jackson opened the driver's-side door and climbed into the vehicle, balancing two large cups of ice cream.

"If he remembered everything I told him, he should be wired up and ready to go," Jackson said, handing over my ice cream. Then he chuckled and added, "For some reason he didn't want me to tape the stuff on his chest."

As if on cue, Mr. Jonas's shouting voice came through the speakers. "I can't believe I made this bet with you. But Abe Jonas makes good on his bets, no matter what."

Knowing he couldn't hear us, Jackson and I laughed. He and Mr. Jonas had made a wager before Jackson and I went to Germany, and I only learned about it after we got back. If we came home without any useful info for the case, Jackson would become the newest attendee of Gray Is Great, the Tuesday night Zumba class. He would be wired and taped so Mr. Jonas could watch and make fun of him. If Jackson and I succeeded on our Germany mission, it would be a return trip to Zumba class for Mr. Jonas.

For many reasons, I felt grateful we didn't come back with nothing, though a part of me would have loved to see Jackson dance it up with those ladies. As it worked out, though, Mr. Jonas was going back into the Zumba lair. And just to make things a bit more interesting, we told him how much Geraldine enjoyed his last visit to Zumba class.

It was the same technical setup as before: we could hear and see everything on the laptop computer in Jackson's car. He made a few more adjustments, and the picture quality improved to a crisp image. We settled back into our seats, ready to tuck into our ice cream and enjoy the show.

Mr. Jonas had finished adjusting his clothing and appeared to be gathering himself before walking into Gladys's exercise studio. He didn't have too long, though because class would begin in a few minutes.

"I want you both to know," he said quietly, "if that woman shows up on my doorstep, you're in serious trouble."

He took another couple of deep breaths and got out of his truck. It was dusk but Jackson and I could see the cars in the parking lot. It appeared everyone would be there. These ladies did love their Zumba.

Gladys greeted Mr. Jonas at the door. "Abe, we are delighted to have you back. The ladies will be so surprised to see you—they were sure we had scared you off last time."

Mr. Jonas muffled a defeated groan and took Gladys's extended hand. I watched her face as she led him to the Zumba room. I knew what was behind her enthusiastic smile—loss and heartache. We agreed in the interrogation room that we'd keep each other's secrets: I'd say nothing about her past, and she wouldn't divulge my identity as the secret obituary writer. But there was more than this agreement between us—we were becoming friends who wanted to understand each other.

Screams erupted as Mr. Jonas entered the dance room, and for a moment all we could see was a jumble of leopard and lace and sequins.

"Look who has come back to us," said Gladys, somewhat after the fact. I could barely hear her over the five screaming Zumba dancers.

"I just knew you'd come back. I could tell we made a connection last time. Didn't you feel it?" Geraldine sounded breathy with excitement.

Jackson and I tried to muffle our laughter, not wanting to miss a word.

"All I remember is hitting the floor with my face," Mr. Jonas said sarcastically. Not the answer Geraldine was hoping for, but she pressed on, undaunted.

"If you like, you can come to my house and I'll teach you a few dance moves. I could make your Zumba experience so much more fulfilling." She said the last part in a husky whisper. I pictured Dean Tolman spying on Geraldine practicing her Zumba in her basement, his imagination going wild.

"Do you have a basement?" Curiosity and fear filled Mr. Jonas's voice.

"Yes!" answered Geraldine. "How did you know?"

"I think I'd better not come over." His response was drowned out by the loud salsa music as class began.

I settled in to enjoy the ice cream, Mr. Jonas's adventure, and just spending time with Jackson.

As we watched Geraldine wrap her leopard scarf around my boss's neck and pull him across the dance floor, I couldn't help but wonder if anything would come from her relentless pursuit of him. Imagining them as a couple made me laugh to myself.

I scraped the bottom of my ice cream cup and put it on the dashboard. And although Jackson was only halfway through his, I took his cup from him and set it next to mine. Then I leaned over and kissed him soundly.

The salsa music on the laptop faded away.

If you like funny stuff, cool books, and puppy pictures,
sign up for Amy Martinsen's newsletter
at http://www.goawayimreading.com.

About the Author

Amy Martinsen received a bachelor of arts in English education from Arizona State University, and a master of arts in English from Northern Arizona University. She is the author of *Hints for Latter-day Saints' Golden Years* (2019) and *Marriage Hints for LDS Newlyweds* (2018), as well as the novels *Changing Worlds* (2015), *The Secret Obituary Writer* (first published in 2016), and *The Secret Obituary Writer: Book Two* (2019). *The Secret Obituary Writer* was nominated for a 2016 Whitney Award. In 2017, a popular blogger selected Amy as one of the Top Ten LDS Authors You Need to Read. Amy wrote the short story "Lilly's Photograph" (Moose Enterprise, 2002) and the article "The Tower of Babel and the Teaching of Grammar: Writing Instruction for a New Century," published in the September 2000 *English Journal*. Readers can learn more about Amy and her books, as well as sign up for her newsletter, at goawayimreading.com.

If you enjoyed *The Secret Obituary Writer,* you'll love *The Secret Obituary Writer: Book Two.*

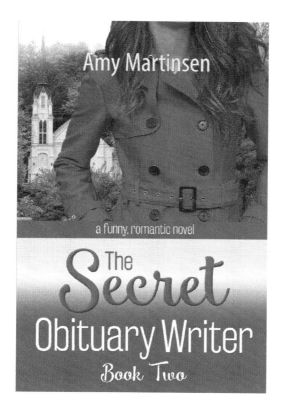

Lizzy and Jackson's story continues. Will Lizzy's job stay a secret? Will Lizzy and Jackson's love flourish? And what about Mr. Jonas? Find out in *The Secret Obituary Writer: Book Two.*